Seeing Emily

Seeing Emily

JOYCE LEE WONG

Amulet Books
New York

Library of Congress Cataloging-in-Publication Data:
Lee Wong, Joyce.
Seeing Emily / by Joyce Lee Wong.
p. cm.
Summary: Relates in free verse the experiences of sixteen-year-old Emily, a
gifted artist and the daughter of immigrants to the United States, as she tries
to reconcile her American self with her Chinese heritage.
ISBN 0-8109-5757-4
[1. Self-perception—Fiction. 2. Chinese Americans—Fiction. 3. Family
life—Fiction. 4. Artists—Fiction. 5. High schools—Fiction. 6. Schools—
Fiction.] I. Title.

PZ7.L51514See 2005
[Fic]—dc22
2005011608

copyright © 2005 Joyce Lee Wong

Designed by Jay Colvin

Printed and bound in Canada
10 9 8 7 6 5 4 3 2 1

AMULET

Published in 2005 by Amulet Books,
an imprint of Harry N. Abrams, Inc.
100 Fifth Avenue
New York, NY 10011
www.abramsbooks.com

Abrams is a subsidiary of

LA MARTINIÈRE

For Bill, Liam, and Sasha,
and for my parents,
Yuan-Wu Chow Lee
and Chi-Chang Lee,
with love

Acknowledgments

I extend heartfelt thanks to Susan Van Metre, Andrea Colvin, Sonia Levitin, Susan Goldman Rubin, Agnes S. C. Wang, Margaret Wang, Mei-ling Chen, Yun Wang, Howard Chia, John Hopkins, Priscilla and Jennifer Wong, the PEN Center USA West, the Society of Children's Book Writers and Illustrators Ventura/Santa Barbara Chapter, and the University of California at Los Angeles Extension Writers' Program. Special thanks to Ming-Qian, Ming-Shan, and Ming-Fang.

Seeing Emily

1. Golden Palace

FLIRTING

It was Saturday night
at our restaurant, Golden Palace,
the only Chinese restaurant
in our town outside Richmond.
It was just past seven
and the dining room was nearly full.
As Mama seated two customers
in a corner booth, she caught my eye.
I nodded and headed back to the kitchen
for a fresh pot of tea.

I was pouring the tea,
a sweet steaminess
rising from the hot metal pot
and traces of white vapor

disappearing into the air above the teacups,
when one of the customers
in the booth asked me,
"Which would you recommend,
the kung-pao chicken
or the chicken with snow peas?"

Looking up from the teapot,
I gave my attention to a couple
a few years older than me,
college students perhaps.
The girl, slim
with short brown hair,
was looking down at the menu.
2   The boy was dark-haired
and hazel-eyed,
extremely good-looking.

Looking at him,
I could almost feel my pupils enlarge,
dark circles blooming out,
the better to take him in.
Studying the contours
of his cheekbones,
the curve of his mouth,
and his eyes, amber-brown,
I thought how much
I'd like to paint his face.

•   •   •

Realizing I was staring,
I felt my own face redden.
But he only continued
to smile at me,
waiting for my response.

He regarded me
with an expression
so friendly and warm,
almost intimate.
I caught
my breath,
forgetting his question.
"What?" I said.

He smiled again,
his look so easy and open
I felt a loose, light smile
spread across my face
as though I were a sunflower
turning bold bright rays
and deep cushiony center
up toward the sun.

"Xiao-jie!" Mama's voice in my ear
made me jump.
I hadn't heard her approach.
She continued in Chinese,
"What are you doing,

flirting with a customer?
Smiling like that,
showing all your teeth."
She shook her head, frowning as though
I'd exposed much more
than my teeth.

Mama took the teapot,
then thrust a plastic bag toward me,
saying, *"The Chos brought this. Put it away*
in the kitchen, hao bu hao?"
Although she framed it as a question
it was more a direction than a request.
Mama pushed the bag into my hands
then turned to the customers.
In English she asked them,
"May I take your order?"

I stood motionless
for a moment, stunned
by Mama's interruption and scolding,
her quick dismissal.
How could she treat me this way
in front of other people,
especially this boy?
As I recalled her tone,
her suggestion that I'd behaved improperly,
even immorally,
a rising anger pounded

in my chest,
pulsing through my temples.

Listening to Mama
chatting pleasantly with the customers,
I bit back the hot words gathering in my mouth
and strode away,
the carpeted floor
quieting my steps.

Pulling apart the handles
of the plastic bag I was holding,
I looked inside and saw
a pink cardboard bakery box
marked with familiar Chinese characters.
Moon cakes, I thought.
The Chos, Baba and Mama's friends from Taiwan,
gave us moon cakes every September,
and the festive bakery box
in my hands made me remember that
both Mid-Autumn Festival
and my sixteenth birthday
were next week.

As I headed for the kitchen,
I heard Baba's voice ring out.
I glanced back toward the cash register
and saw him saying good-bye
to some regular customers,

the tenor music of his laugh
reaching me from across the room.

Golden Palace

Don't go into the restaurant business,
Baba says, the hours are long
the work is *ku, bitter,*
and the better business is,
the harder you work.

Baba thought our restaurant
would do well in this neighborhood.

Business isn't bad,
but it's hard to find a chef around here
who knows wok cooking.
So Baba, Mama, and I often cook.

The kitchen's always hotter
than an August afternoon.
Oil crackles and spits
when you drop chopped
vegetables and meat
into the waiting wok.
Over the sizzling din,
the sharp scrape of metal on metal
as you stir-fry slabs of chicken or beef,
then chunks of tofu, slices of bamboo,

pea pods and water chestnuts,
always keeping the pieces moving
over the rippling, flaming heat.

With the oil in the wok
at 375 degrees for deep-frying,
you try to be careful,
but sometimes on a busy weekend night,
when the roar of the customers' conversation
follows you into the kitchen,
and your feet start to tire
and your back and arms complain
but the orders keep coming fast,
hot oil can leap up, lightning-quick toward you,
spattering your clothing or skin;
we've all been burned in the kitchen.

7 ⌒

Not Calling Alex Huang

I was putting away the moon cakes
in the restaurant's kitchen
when Mama walked in behind me.
She lit the gas beneath the wok,
and asked, "Have you called Alex Huang?"

She added strips of marinated beef
to the oil warming in the wok,
then looked pointedly at me,

as though she were reminding me to finish
a homework assignment long undone.
Mama's question grated
like the sudden sharp squeal of the spatula's edge
as she scraped it against the wok.

"Who?" I said blankly,
though I knew perfectly well whom she meant.
I was still burning
from the way she'd embarrassed me
in front of the dark-haired boy.

Mama gave me an exasperated look.
"Don't you remember, I told you about
Mrs. Huang, my college classmate,
and her son who's transferring
to your school next week?"

"Emily?" Mama's voice rose above
the sounds of fresh sizzling
as she sprinkled pieces of broccoli
and carrots into the wok.

"Yes," I said. "I *remember*."
How could I forget
when she'd been asking me to call him
every single day for a week?
Mama had asked me to help him
get settled in at school.

• • •

I knew it would be hard for anyone
to start their sophomore year
at a new high school,
two weeks into the semester.
Mama said it would be
especially difficult for Alex
since he'd moved with his parents
from Taiwan to Maryland
only two years ago,
and now he'd be switching schools again.

I should have called him,
but somehow, every time I thought about doing it,
I ended up getting distracted,
busying myself with something else
until it was too late to call.

Now I looked away from Mama,
focusing instead on a curve of water
shining on a freshly washed plate.
I concentrated on carefully
wiping it dry.

"You didn't do it, did you?" Mama said.

I was about to admit I hadn't.
I was even going to apologize
when Mama said sharply, "I asked you to,

and you said you would,
but you never did."
She punctuated her words
with firm, quick shakes of her wrist,
as she sprinkled the wok's contents with soy sauce.
A few dark droplets stung the hot metal sides,
hissing in protest as they
writhed and sputtered, whitening
until they evaporated into tiny wisps of smoke.

Suddenly, anger flared,
quick as the flames
licking at the bottom of the wok.
The lie exploded from my mouth,

startling me.
"I did call him!" I said,
sounding so self-righteous,
I nearly believed myself.

It was almost as though
I were listening to someone else speak
as the words came rushing out.
"I talked to him," I heard myself say.
"And I'm going to meet him at school
to show him around."

Mama studied me for a moment, then said,
"You'll show him where his classes are?
And introduce him to his teachers
and your friends?"

. . .

I nodded.
The lie sat uneasily in my stomach
like an extra piece of cake
I hadn't been able to resist eating
even though I was already full.
I thought I would burst
from the queasy pressure
in my gut, and I was sure
Mama would notice
my discomfort.

Instead, as she appraised me,
her expression softened.
"Hao," she said, *Good.*
Her approval was like
a forkful of frosting
swirled thickly along the tines,
its sugary sweetness
too much to bear.

I hadn't meant to lie to Mama.
I was also afraid she'd talk to Mrs. Huang
and discover the truth.
Even if Mrs. Huang didn't call her
sometime soon, I knew Mama would want
to invite the Huangs over for dinner
before too long.

Now I watched the fire beneath the wok

dance orange and blue,
flaming high in a final, ecstatic burst
before Mama shut off the gas.
I blinked and saw,
against my closed lids,
burning spots of gold,
and for a moment it felt
as if my eyes had turned
yellow as a cat's.

I imagined I was a cat,
her eyes shining
as she watches a goldfish
that shimmers on the floor.
12   The fish jerks and flips,
thrashing from side to side,
its body heaving
and gills straining
as it fights for breath.

As she tracks its every movement,
the cat's tail lashes
and her hackles rise,
so the fur on her back and neck
stiffens.

Licking at the water
still clinging to her paw,
the cat feels something like regret,

for batting the fish from its bowl.
Then, with a final flick of her tail,
she turns her back and exits the room,
silently slipping outside.

"Don't forget to tell Alex *hello*
for me and Baba," Mama said now,
as she transferred the beef and broccoli
to a dinner plate for me to serve.

I nodded, but couldn't meet her eyes.
I placed the steaming dish on my serving tray
then walked quickly out to the dining room,
the kitchen doors swinging shut behind me.

The Kiss

It was after eight thirty
and the restaurant was still half full.
Mama refilled a family's water glasses
while I cleared dirty dishes from another table,
stacking them in a deep plastic bin.
I looked over toward the corner booth
and saw the dark-haired boy
pull a few bills from his wallet
and place them on the table.
As he and the girl stood up to leave,
he gave her a smile. He placed

his hand on her shoulder,
walking slightly behind her
as they headed for the door.

The bells atop the door clanged
when the boy held it open,
and the girl glanced up, startled.
She made a face,
laughing at herself,
then looked up and smiled
at the dark-haired boy.
With one hand still on the door,
he moved his other hand
down to her back,
pulled her slightly closer
and leaned down
to give her
a kiss.

A plate slipped
from my fingers,
clattering loudly against
the other dishes in the bin.
Startled, I looked up
to see Mama's expression of surprise.
I straightened the plate
then said, "It didn't break."
Mama studied me for a moment
without speaking.

She looked as if she had more to say,
but she only said,
"Be more careful next time."

The Last Thing I Wanted

As I headed from the kitchen
to clear another table,
the bells atop the front door jingled,
signaling the entrance of new customers.
It was a Chinese family,
a middle-aged couple
and a boy about my age.

He wore glasses
and a short-sleeved shirt
tucked into corduroy pants
that rode high enough to expose
the large, padded tongue
and neatly tied laces
of his white tennis shoes.

I wasn't surprised to hear Baba
speak to these customers in Chinese.
Smiling broadly, he came around
from the cash register and said,
"How did you know where to find us?"
• • •

Smiling back, the woman said,
"When we decided to go out for Chinese food,
we thought this might be your restaurant."

"Indeed it is," Baba said.
"It's wonderful to see you all again."
He shook the man's hand, then turned to the boy
and clapped him on the shoulder.
"Can this be Alex? You've grown so tall!"

Alex? The name caused me to shiver
as if a trickle of cold water
were running down my back—
How strange for Alex Huang to show up.

The coolness tingled along the back of my neck
and prickled on my scalp,
and I wondered if I were being punished
somehow for my lie.

I wanted to disappear,
or at least to retreat as quickly as I could.
They hadn't seen me yet,
and I thought I might be able to make it
back into the kitchen before anyone noticed me.

But then Baba looked in my direction
with an expression so stern
I felt chilled.
He knows about the lie, I thought.

I tried to relax
my mouth into a smile,
but I felt my own guilt
naked on my face
and my feet were rooted to the carpet.

I felt like a cat,
caught in the middle of the street
she was trying to cross,
startled by the roar of an oncoming car
speeding directly toward her.

Baba scanned the room,
meeting my eyes.
He held my glance and smiled,
waving me over,
and I gave him a weak smile back.

The cat's first instinct
is to freeze in place,
crouching down low,
trying to hide,
and hoping against hope
that the car might
somehow
vanish.

Just behind me I heard Mama's gasp
of pleased surprise. *"Oh, look who's here!"*

She put her hand on my arm
and pulled me forward.

I felt blinded
as if from the overwhelming glare
of headlights, my eyes
two bright spots
reflecting back shafts of light.
I was unable to turn away,
and escape was
impossible.

I clenched and unclenched
fingers gone numb.
With my heart thudding in my ears,
I walked ahead of Mama,
straight toward Baba
and
the Huangs.

"Emily, say hello to the Huangs," Mama said,
nudging me toward the table.

"Hello Auntie and Uncle Huang," I said
in a strange, tinny voice
that didn't sound like my own.

Mama clasped her friends' hands,
then put her arm around their son's shoulders.

"Emily tells me you've met over the phone,"
she said to Alex.

Alex looked from Mama to me,
a puzzled expression on his face.
But he didn't say anything
to contradict her.

My face felt frozen into
a parody of a smile.
I listened helplessly as Mama continued,
"She says the two of you
will be getting together this week at school."

She turned to me and asked,
"What day are you going to meet Alex?"

My heartbeat was like
the thunder of an oncoming car,
so near it caused the ground
beneath my feet to shake.

"What?" I said in English, stalling for time.

Mama frowned slightly at me.
She turned to the Huangs and said apologetically,
"Emily's Chinese is terrible."

She switched to English and said to me,

"I *asked* you, 'When are you and Alex
getting together?'"

I didn't know which annoyed me more,
Mama's assumption that my Chinese was so poor
I couldn't understand such a simple question,
or the way she'd felt the need to apologize for me.

Alex looked again
from Mama to me,
then opened his mouth to speak.

Alarm crackled through me,
as though I were a cat
with fur bristling
and ears pushed back,
her eyes round and dark
with dread.

She knows her only chance
for survival
is to force her limbs into motion
and to make the terrifying, endless dash
for the other side of the street.
Somehow, she finds herself
moving forward
with a tremendous burst of speed,
running for
her life.

• • •

Before Alex could say anything,
I said, "On Thursday,"
my voice cracking on the word.
I cleared my throat and repeated,
"We'll be meeting on Thursday."

Alex met my eyes and smiled.
In English he said, "That will be very nice."

Just then, a customer caught my glance
as he waved in my direction
and lifted his empty glass.
"Drink refill," I said to Mama.

Mama nodded, releasing me.

"It was nice meeting you," I said to the Huangs,
before hurrying off toward the kitchen.

It is no longer fear
but exhilaration the cat feels,
reveling in the power of her limbs
and the knowledge
that freedom
is hers.

But then, as her heartbeat calms
and her fur smooths back down,

the cat pauses to consider
just how close
an escape
it was.

I refilled the drink,
then walked back to the kitchen
for an order of spring rolls.
I glanced back at Mama,
still talking with the Huangs.

Thanks to Alex,
I didn't think Mama would find out
that I'd lied.
And if I showed him around at school,
it would almost make up for the lie.
I probably owed him as much.

"Excuse me."
I'd been so lost in my thoughts
I hadn't heard anyone approach.
Now I looked up and saw Alex,
trying to walk past me
on his way to the bathroom.

We moved toward each other,
then hastily back,
caught in an awkward dance
as each of us tried

to move out of the other's way.
He gave me an embarrassed half-smile,
before finally stepping back
so that I could walk ahead of him.

"I'm sorry," I said,
quickly threading my way between the tables,
clearing the way for him.

I looked back at Alex,
as he walked toward the bathroom.
I noticed a slight cowlick
rising from the back of his head,
the strands of hair bouncing a little
as he went,
and I heard the *zip-zip*
of his corduroy pants,
the sound of the rippled fabric
chafing back and forth
as he walked.

As much as I wished
I could take back my lie,
I knew that helping Alex Huang
get settled in at school
was the last thing
I wanted to do.

NOT YET SEEING

It was after ten thirty
as I cleared the rest of the tables,
carting bins of dirty dishes to the kitchen.
By the time we closed
the restaurant most evenings
my feet were sore and I was ready
to sit down and rest.
But tonight as I walked past the corner booth,
I could almost see
the dark-haired boy.

Remembering the lift of his chin,
his easy smile,
I didn't feel at all tired.
There was a tingle
in my skin, and I felt
the frenetic buzzing of bees,
a languid warmth as if honey
flowed through my veins.

I usually spent an hour or so
drawing or painting
after Baba, Mama, and I
came home from the restaurant.
Tonight, seeking release
for the energy of clover and bees,
I couldn't wait to start drawing.

• • •

I was starting a new assignment
for art class, an interior self-portrait.
The art teacher, Mrs. Burns, had been showing us
paintings by Bonnard and Vuillard,
and our assignment was to create
a self-portrait by drawing
our own bedroom,
a library or gymnasium,
any interior space we might choose
to represent ourselves.

Wheeling the cart of dirty dishes
one final time into the kitchen,
I noticed Baba's cooking apron
hanging from its usual hook.
Despite the pattern of dark stains
and the spatterings of oil marking the cloth,
its folds fell neatly, almost
gracefully toward the floor.
I thought of Baba,
who always seemed to maintain
a steady calmness,
a certain measure of ease
within his surroundings,
even after cooking at the restaurant
all day and night.

After loading the dishwasher
and putting the cart away,

I found the box of moon cakes.
I arranged three cakes on a plate,
two clustered together on one side
and one in the foreground
tipping out toward the viewer.
I pulled out pencil and sketch pad
and began to sketch
the lines of the apron,
the circular forms of the moon cakes,
and behind them the wok on the stove
with cutting board and cooking utensils,
the kitchen counters and exhaust fan.

I felt a presence behind me
as I drew, and I heard
Mama's voice saying, "Is this
for your interior self-portrait?"

I tilted my pad down
so she wouldn't be able to see it
and said, "*Mama.* I haven't even finished
my first *sketch.*"

Mama smiled. "Okay, okay.
Let me see it when you're ready."

Mama left me alone
as I continued to draw,
but her interruption left me

feeling annoyed,
and try as I might,
I couldn't get anything down
that looked right.

Finally, I closed my sketch pad
with a sigh of exasperation.
"Are you ready to go?" Baba asked.
I saw he'd finished cleaning the kitchen
and I nodded.

"Mama's waiting up front," he said.
"Put away the moon cakes
and we'll go home."

Replacing the moon cakes in the box,
I thought about my unsuccessful sketch.
I resolved to look at it again
tomorrow with a fresh eye.
I liked the idea of setting my interior
in the restaurant's kitchen
and I didn't think the composition was at fault.
I knew that I wasn't seeing it yet.

Thinking about truly *seeing*
the kitchen, its space
and the forms within,
I felt my eye honing its focus
and my mind expanding its reach.

It was the way I felt
when I started to draw,
losing myself
in the rhythm of pencil on paper,
watching the forms take shape
and the landscape opening up,
until I felt
I could climb right inside
the world of my drawing.

Cucumber Soup

Even after working all day and night at the Palace,
Mama insists on cooking for us at home.
She cooks food we don't serve at the restaurant,
dishes she ate growing up.
She says it wouldn't feel like home
unless she could cool down the day
with a bowl of cucumber soup,
white circles of cucumber floating in chicken broth
with a dash of wine
and a splash of sesame oil,
slivers of sweet pork, snips of green onion
and tender cubes of tofu
that almost melt away in your spoon.

Tonight, I couldn't finish my serving.
Watching me eating more and more slowly

until I put down my spoon,
Mama frowned.
"You usually eat two bowls of soup," she said.

I wasn't sure how to explain it.
It was something like waking up one day
and realizing
you no longer want to listen
to the songs you've always loved.
Instead, you're yearning
for something new.

"Are you feeling okay?" Mama asked,
and her look of worry
jarred me
like a sudden,
discordant note.

"I'm *fine*," I said.

DRAWING WITH MAMA

I remembered a certain third-grade day
when nothing seemed to go right.
That morning I had to stay in from recess
writing *I will not talk in class* one hundred times.
At lunch they ran out of ice cream
just when it was my turn in line,

and during P.E., I dropped the kick ball,
allowing the other team to score.

When I came home from school,
Mama took one look at my face
and asked me what was wrong.

I shook my head in response,
and Mama led me to the kitchen.
I settled myself
in one of our dark wooden chairs,
hooking my feet around
the legs of my chair.
I noticed how knobby

my ankles and feet felt,
rubbing against the cool wood.
When Mama asked
if I'd like a snack,
I shook my head again.

Mama studied me for a moment,
then asked me
if I wanted to draw.
I shrugged,
and she asked if I'd like her
to draw along with me.

When I nodded,
Mama set up our first still life

for the two of us to draw together.
She draped a sheet over the table
bunching it here and there
to make wrinkles and folds.
On the table she placed
our green clay bowl
with its sides flared like a calla lily
and its bottom spiraled like a snail's shell;
two Mason canning jars,
one standing upright
the other tipped to its side;
and the kitchen hand broom
for its bristly texture.
She added our tea kettle,
the watering can,
and even a fallen branch
from our backyard dogwood tree,
winter-smooth
and bare of leaves.

Watching Mama sketch,
her pencil lines
light but sure
as they traced the curve of a bowl
and followed the shape of the branch
slightly bowed
and casting a snake-like shadow
across the crinkled sheet beneath,
I wanted to draw

the same things as Mama,
hoping I, too
could make a scene take shape
with such life and grace
as it filled the white of the page.

Mama said
I should draw the still life
from a different perspective,
choose my own objects to include,
and create my own scene to draw,
but nothing I picked on my own
seemed quite as enticing
as what Mama was drawing.

So she smiled and told me
even if I sat
exactly where she did,
and even if I drew
the same things she drew
they would become my own things
in my own drawing.

She had me stand on her chair
to see the objects from her viewpoint
and then had me move
back to my own seat.
"Can you see," she said,
"how the perspective changes,

that the bowl viewed from your seat
appears more top-heavy?
Do you see the way
the branch seems bigger
and casts a different shadow
when seen from your place?"

Mama always praised my drawings,
the texture of my branch
the roundness of my bowl,
and her words were sweet
like the red-bean filling
she prepared for *bao zi* dumplings.
After the praise
the teaching would come.
I didn't mind, I even liked
hearing Mama's suggestions.
Her voice was so patient
and full of care when she said,
"Ni kan. Look, Emily.
Let me show you . . ."

After I made the changes
I could see how much better
they made my drawings
and when Mama said,
"Zhen hao. You've done
a fine job, Emily,"
these words were like

the *bao zi* dumplings
the two of us made together.
I'd look across the kitchen table
and see Mama
filling the doughy circles
with red-bean paste,
while I pressed spoonfuls
of lotus-seed filling
inside my own dumplings.
Together we pinched the circles closed
then steamed the buns
until they were tender and soft,
each bite just the right blend
of rich filling and dough—

the *bao zi* dumplings
Mama and I made
together
were sweet indeed.

RESTAURANT DRAWING

All day Sunday, I worked on the restaurant drawing.
In the morning I made sketches at the restaurant,
during the afternoon and evening
I was at home, working on the drawing itself.

I was so lost in my drawing that night,
it startled me to hear the scrape of keys in the door,

the familiar heavy click of the bolt sliding back,
the off-key music of the door swinging open.
Baba and Mama were home.
I called out *Hello,*
and heard my parents' answering voices.

I looked at the clock,
it was after ten.
I couldn't believe how quickly
the time had passed.
I looked back at my drawing,
nearly finished now,
and heard footsteps coming up the stairs.
Mama appeared in my doorway
and asked, "Would you like a snack?
Baba's cutting some melon now."

"Maybe after I finish this," I said.
Mama looked over at my drawing,
then came into the room for a better look.
She studied it for a long moment,
then smiled. "You really worked hard
on this piece," she said.

"I can almost reach out and touch this cloth,"
Mama continued. "The wrinkles and folds
are so beautifully drawn.
You got Baba's apron just right."
She smiled at me and added,

"It looks like it could use
a little more washing though,
doesn't it?"

I laughed,
pleased by her praise.

She continued to study my drawing,
staying quiet for so long that I asked
somewhat warily, "What?"

Mama hesitated for a moment,
then said, "Isn't this supposed to be a self-portrait?"

"It's *supposed* to be," I said stiffly.

"For a self-portrait," Mama continued,
"it seems a little . . . dark. This is a daytime scene
and the restaurant's kitchen is actually quite bright.
But your drawing shows it as a dim room
with heavy overtones. Looking at it makes me want
to open a window, to let in fresh air and light."

When I didn't respond, Mama said,
"What do you think?"

I shrugged. "Maybe I'm a dark, stuffy person."

Mama gave me a look. "Emily."

Switching to Chinese, she said,
"Ni bu yao zhe ge yang zi,"
Don't be like this.
"I'm telling you this to help you.
Other people may say only sweet things
to flatter you, but I'm your mother
and I tell you the truth.
It's for your own good."

Staring down at my drawing,
I could feel Mama's eyes on me.
Finally she sighed and said,
"I'm going down to have some tea.
You're welcome to come, too."

Even the sound of Mama's footsteps
receding down the stairs
nettled me, each soft thud,
the familiar squeak as she
reached the second-to-last stair.

I knew I sounded defensive,
even to my own ears,
but for once I didn't want to listen
to Mama telling me how to draw.
It was *my* drawing after all,
and I wanted to figure
things out for myself.

• • •

From the kitchen,
the tea kettle sang out,
the notes of its high-pitched song
rising to a frantic crescendo
before it was suddenly squelched.
I heard a final indignant squeal
issue from the kettle
as Mama took it from the burner
to pour the water for tea.

More sounds wafted up,
the clink of forks against plates,
the low murmur of my parents' voices.
Next I heard
the crackling of plastic,
followed by the snip of scissors
and the sharp snap of elastic
against cardboard,
the sounds of Mama opening
the box of moon cakes.

I could almost feel the puff
of bakery-fragrant air
as she pushed back the lid,
and the heady scent
of freshly baked moon cakes
reached me from downstairs.

Smelling lotus seed and red-bean paste,

I felt carefree and light.
I gave myself over to
a simple, childlike joy,
lost in savoring the fragrance
and anticipating the taste
of the cakes.

Moon Cake, Chocolate Cake

On my fifth birthday,
Baba cut the moon cake
into three parts,
his knife pushing down
into golden pastry top, sinking
into sweet bean filling,
piercing the whole
egg yolk in the center.
Next the blade
struck the plate,
ding. It was
Mid-Autumn Festival,
the same day as my birthday.

Mama said it was lucky
to be born on a day
when the round moon
glowed, full and bright
like our family.

We savored
the moon cake:
rich bites of dark
bean paste, mixed with
thick, sweet crust
and salty yellow yolk.

Later that night, Mama lit
five candles on my birthday cake,
throwing an orange glow
over the frosted words,
Happy Birthday, Emily.
Baba and Mama urged me
to make a wish.

But what to wish for?
I thought and thought, as
my cheeks stretched tight
with air and I blew
with all my might.
Still I thought,
while the flames danced
then fluttered out, even
as smoke wafted up
rising in lazy spirals,
mixing with the sounds
of Baba and Mama cheering
and clapping, our laughter
ringing out through the kitchen.

• • •

And suddenly,
through the slightly smoky air
and the buttery sweet
smell of cake, I knew this:
I was too happy
to wish for
anything more.

II. The Mural

PORTRAITS

Monday at school,
at lunch with Nina Cooper and Liz Phelps,
my best friends since junior high.
Small and energetic,
Nina reminded me of a robin
with her friendly, inquisitive look.
Liz was thin, and as tall
as many of the boys in our grade,
but she never slouched
to make herself seem shorter.

Today Liz seemed subdued,
but less so with Nina than me.
I wondered whether Liz was still
thinking about our last English test,
handed back to us on Friday.
I hadn't wanted to tell her my grade,

but she wouldn't stop asking
until I admitted it was an A.
From the look on her face when I told her,
anyone could imagine she hadn't
scored as well herself.
But only someone
who knew her as well as I did
might have guessed she'd probably made
an A- on her own test.

Since we'd started our sophomore year,
Liz seemed even more focused
on academics than before. I wondered
if her parents were pressuring her
to keep her grades up.
I knew she wouldn't feel like
talking about it now, so I decided
to bring it up another time.

"Hey, you guys," I said now,
"Can I show you my drawing?"

"Sure, show it to us!" Nina said.
Liz nodded and I took out
the restaurant drawing I'd finished last night.

Nina's eyes widened
and she drew in her breath.
"Wow, Emily," she said admiringly.

• • •

"It's perfect," Liz said
in a tone of mock-disgust,
". . . as usual." She spoke
as though she were kidding,
but there was a note
of sarcasm in her voice
that surprised me.

I heard an answering edge
to my own voice as I said coolly,
"But does it look like a self-portrait?"

Nina looked from Liz to me,
then put her hand on my arm
and said, "It looks like the portrait
of someone who really enjoys eating."
She gave me a nudge and added,
"I think it looks just like you."

I laughed with everyone else,
then took another look at my portrait.
Mama was right, I thought,
it *was* a dark drawing. Could this reflect
some aspect of myself?
People sometimes describe me
as serious, and I suppose I am.
I certainly don't have Nina's
sunny and easygoing nature,
much as I wish I did.

And it's true these days
I've been feeling moody.
Maybe this is why Liz and I
haven't been getting along so well.

"If you were in Emily's art class,"
Nina asked Liz, "what room
would you pick for your self-portrait?"

Without hesitation Liz said,
"I'd draw my own room."
Liz's bedroom centered around
her computer work station.
She'd set it up like an office,
complete with wraparound desk
and filing cabinets, neat caddies
stocked with supplies.

I imagined Liz's portrait,
busy with sharp angles and quick lines,
alive with geometric shapes,
her computer monitor, keyboard, and mouse
a network of fluid rectangles and curves,
her rolling desk chair
a series of ovals and circles
sleek as a mount
impatient for its rider.
The air itself would hum,
restlessly waiting for Liz

to spin shapes into motion
and send well-oiled gears and wheels
whirring and turning until
the room throbbed into life.

"I wish we were doing interior portraits
in my art class," Nina said.

"If you were," I said,
"which room would you draw?"

She thought for a moment then said,
"I'd draw a kitchen, too.
Not the one at my house now,
but the kitchen I'd like to have one day
if I could design my own house."
In a soft voice she added,
"I think the kitchen should be comfortable,
you know, *cozy*,
a place that brings people together."

For Nina's portrait,
I envisioned a watercolor,
its background a window
opening out to washes of green and blue,
a sea of trees reaching up
into an expanse of sky.
Nestled against the window,
a wooden table with chairs

pulled slightly out from the table,
inviting you in.
A diagonal panel of sun
slants down from the glass panes
to splash the table and chairs with light,
warming the wood orange-rose
and illuminating a flurry
of glimmering dust motes
as they dance their slow dance
through the air.

I turned from thoughts of Nina's portrait
back to my own drawing.
I found it easy to imagine myself in it,
working in the restaurant's kitchen.
Unbidden, my parents' images appeared,
joining me there,
Baba deep-frying spring rolls
and Mama chopping scallions for soup.
Once again my eye was drawn
to the lines of Baba's apron,
the moon cakes' circular shapes,
and I heard an echo of Mama's voice
asking me to put them away.

Suddenly I realized I'd made
more of a family portrait
than a self-portrait.

• • •

At that moment
an image appeared
in my mind,
a bird
molting her feathers,
shaking off her winter garb
and exchanging it
for new plumage,
giddy and bright
as the stirrings
of spring.

A breeze
teases the air,
and the bird stretches her wings,
feeling the tantalizing lift of current
as she poises at the edge
of her nest.

Ready to dive into
the dazzling expanse
of air and light,
the bird envisions herself
soaring higher
and higher until
the very world seems to shrink
beneath the sweep
of her wings.

CHOSEN FOR THE MURAL

When I turned in my restaurant drawing,
Mrs. Burns smiled.
"Echoes of Cézanne," she said,
knowing how much I love his work.
The next thing she said was even better.
She asked me to work on a mural
for the school's front hallway.
"It will be a showpiece," she said.
"This mural needs two strong painters
so I thought of you.
Will you do it?"

~ 50

I smiled and told her, *yes.*
Pleasure sparkled through me
like club soda fizzing in a glass,
my excitement like bubbles
rising up above the rim.
But then I realized
Mrs. Burns said *two* painters.
I wanted to ask her
if I could work with Nina
but she said, "I've also asked Alex Huang
to work on the mural,
and he said yes."

The name *Alex Huang*
was completely unexpected,

like someone behind you stepping down hard,
crushing the back of your shoe
while you're walking,
making you hobble to a stop right there
with your shoe swinging loosely from your toes,
exposing your naked heel.
Seeing my surprise, Mrs. Burns said,
"Alex is a new student.
Today's his first day here.
He showed me some of his work this morning
and I was very impressed.
Have you met Alex yet?"

Have I met Alex Huang?
Mama herself
couldn't have planned it better.

Already I could hear
the slap of brush mixing paint,
see the first splash of color on white,
feel the bristles bending up then down
as I painted the mural's
great waiting face.
But why did it have to be
Alex Huang,
with those thick glasses
and corduroy pants,
the no-name tennis shoes
and faltering English,

that *accent*
with its forced consonants, lilting vowels,
and funny, off-beat
intonation?

Mrs. Burns was saying how glad she was
to have me and Alex painting the mural.
"I think the two of you," she said,
"will work well together."
Hearing this was a double surprise
like suddenly wondering
whether the person who stepped on your heel
made your shoe come off on purpose.
Did Mrs. Burns pair me with him

because we're both Chinese
and she imagines we're somehow alike?

It's true I've never really talked with him,
but I can't believe
we'd have much in common.
After all, I was born here
and he wasn't.
But I wanted to paint
this mural so badly
I didn't say anything about it.

I wondered
just what kind
of an artist

Alex Huang was.
When I asked Mrs. Burns
she laughed and said,
You'll see.

CHANT

My mother is *Chi*-nese
(Slant your eyes up),
My father is *Jap*-anese
(Down, pull 'em down),
I have *dirty* knees
(Stab your fingers at your knees),
My sister has *bigger* these
(Jab those thumbs at your chest)!

"Your father isn't
Japanese," Mama said
when I recited the chant
I learned in first grade.
Mama spoke with
mouth tightened,
brow puckered,
her eyes shining
with something
I'd never seen
before.

• • •

Suddenly
I felt a chill
as if from winter air
when you step out
of the shower,
naked and wet.
I didn't know
exactly what it was
I'd said
to make Mama
look at me
like that
but
I was sorry,
really sorry
even before
Baba
put down his newspaper,
with a rustle-snap,
loud,
loud in a room
so
suddenly
quiet.

Baba's eyes were trained
on me, his face
still, the corners
of his mouth

turned down
as though he'd just tasted
toast burnt black.
His voice whipped out
catching me full
across my
face.
To this day,
my cheeks still burn,
remembering
the way
he said,
spitting out
each word
like
bitter
dry
crumbs,
"Don't
say that,
Emily.
Don't *you*
say
that
again."

THE NEW JUNIOR

Tuesday morning
on my way to history class
I overheard a girl from my homeroom
say, "That's the new junior,
his name's Nick Hancock."
The brightness in her tone
and the way her voice quickened
made me look up.
The boy she pointed out was tall
with a runner's build,
long-legged and lean.
His wheat-pale hair

fell over his forehead
and he ran one hand carelessly
back through his hair
in an unthinking gesture,
surprisingly graceful.
Even in the frenzied
hustle of the hallway,
his pace was relaxed, unhurried.
Something about the way he moved
with a certain sleekness
made me think of a lion
walking slowly, even lazily
through the veldt, yet with
razor-keen senses aware
of the merest change in wind, ever-alert
for the scent of game.

• • •

Just then, a girl walking in front of me
called out, *Nick!*
and he looked in our direction
and smiled, his eyes
burning blue
as the Indian summer
sky outside.
As I watched,
he arched an eyebrow
and his lips curved up
in an easy, teasing grin.

A sudden bump to my shoulder
dislodged the strap of my backpack.
As I turned to pull it back up
a group of kids passed by,
blocking my view of him.
By the time the crowd thinned
he was gone
and I was left
remembering
the sky-bright blue of his eyes,
the heat of his smile.

BAMBOO

Alex Huang's painting:

A grove of bamboo,
spring-green leaves
slender and shapely
as so many small fish
swimming among stalks
thrusting up toward sky
in a pattern of vertical lines
fluid and rhythmic as music,
the supple columns burnished
a rich purple-black,

the slimmer shafts glowing
grass green or cider gold,
wood gleaming
as if polished flute-smooth.

As I continued to look
at this painting
I could almost hear
the rustle of leaves
lifting here and there
as if a breeze were pushing through.
I felt a dark coolness,
smelled wetness and earth,
trees and leaves
filtering light and sound,

filling me with
a sense of peace.

Meeting Alex Huang

After seeing his painting
I wondered if I'd see something different
about Alex Huang, some inner spark
shining through, a hint
of the artist within.
But when we met in the art room
Thursday afternoon,
he looked exactly the same,
smiling back at me almost shyly
as he returned my greeting.

When I told him how much
I liked his painting, he looked back at me
and I saw the art room reflected
shadowy and pale in his glasses.
Light winked across the lenses
as he shook his head and said,
"Oh, no, it's nothing."
The more I told him how good it was,
the more he insisted, *no, really,* it wasn't.

How *Chinese* of him, I thought.

•   •   •

Just then, Mrs. Burns came into the room and said,
"Have you seen Emily's watercolors, Alex?"
"I have," he said. "They're very good."
His voice was quiet, sincere
and unexpectedly it held
a note of authority
that caught me off guard
and I said, "Oh, no
they're not that good."

"You're both so modest," Mrs. Burns said.
She gestured to a stack of art books on the table
and said, "Why don't you take a look at these
and see if anything inspires you for the mural?"

I hid my embarrassment and irritation,
immersing myself
in a book of French artists.
As I flipped through the book,
absorbing colors and forms,
I became aware
of a comfortable quiet
enhanced by small sounds,
the humming of the fluorescent lights above,
the rustling of pages turning,
an occasional crackle
as we looked through the newer books,
releasing the sharp scent of binding and glue
that blended with the smell of the older books,
musty and sweet.

• • •

I came to a reproduction
of Rousseau's *Tiger in a Tropical Storm (Surprised!)*
and admired the jungle grasses and trees,
the rain slanting down,
the tiger crouched below.
"Alex," I said, "Our school mascot's the tiger . . .
What do you think?"

He took the book from me
and looked at the painting for a long moment,
studying it so intently
with an almost palpable concentration
I felt almost as if I were
eavesdropping or staring too long,
and I looked away.

Alex looked up from the book
and nodded thoughtfully. "Yes, I like it."

I thought of Alex's bamboo painting,
and suggested, "Maybe you could start with
the plants, and I could start with the animals . . .
We could show each other our sketches,
and then go from there?"

Alex thought for a moment,
then smiled. "That sounds great."
I saw in his eyes
the same excitement I felt,

the stirring of a new idea,
like the moment before the water boils,
when drifts of steam waft up,
tiny bubbles rise,
the water agitates,
and you know it won't be long
before the water comes to a furious boil,
hot enough to pour
over the leaves,
steeping them until
the water darkens into
a steaming cup
of rich, fragrant tea.

THE IDEAL BOYFRIEND

"I just want someone
I could feel comfortable with," Nina said,
sitting in the cafeteria with me and Liz
at our usual lunch table on Friday.
". . . Someone I could sit down and talk to,
someone who would listen to me."

"I'd want a guy I could relax around
and have a good time with,
without feeling like I always had to be
partying or out doing something
with him all the time . . ."
There was a wistful note

in Nina's voice as she said,
"I guess I'm looking for someone
I could fall in love with."

At that moment
a group of sophomore boys
passed by our table, jostling each other,
laughing and joking loudly.
One poised his hands in the air
as if he were shooting a basketball,
then tossed a half-empty milk carton
into a nearby trash can, where it landed
with a resounding thunk, splattering
droplets of milk outside the can
and making the boys hoot.

Nina looked at the boys and rolled her eyes,
making such a comical face
of combined disbelief and disgust
that we all laughed.
She sighed and added, "I wonder
if a guy like that even exists."

"Anyone I'd want to go out with
would have to love books," Liz said.
Liz had just started dating Marshall Cox,
a tall, lanky junior. Soft-spoken and almost shy,
Marshall seemed totally devoted to Liz.

"Yesterday after school," Liz continued,

"we were at the library and Marshall picked up
a book of Shakespeare's sonnets.
He looked at me and said,
'Shall I compare thee to a summer's day?'"

How corny.
I was about to laugh,
and I saw Nina smile.
But Liz had a faraway look
on her face as she continued,
"'. . . Thou art more lovely and more temperate.'"
Her voice wobbled a little as she spoke
and I studied her closely.

"Liz," I said, surprised, "you're blushing!"

When Liz saw me and Nina grinning at her,
her cheeks grew even pinker.
Recovering, she cleared her throat and said,
"Well, if he didn't appreciate poetry,
I don't see how we could get along at all."

I elbowed Nina
and gave her a look meaning,
Oh, please.

Nina elbowed me back
and gave me a look meaning,
Be nice.

• • •

Just then Liz turned to me and said,
"You're awfully quiet, Emily.
Why don't you tell us about your ideal guy?"
Thoughts of Nick arose,
unbidden, warming
my cheeks.

Watching me, Liz grinned.
"Now look who's blushing."

"I'm not blushing," I said,
feeling my face burn.

Nina smiled slyly and said,
"I don't think Emily's thinking
of any *ideal* guy.
It looks like she has someone
specific in mind."
She grabbed my arm and said,
"Tell us who he is!"

I wanted to tell them,
but I had an odd feeling
I couldn't quite shake.
It was something like being at a party,
and feeling so relaxed
you hear yourself call out,
"Hey, everybody, listen to this!"

• • •

But once everyone stops talking
and looks your way, the waiting silence
suddenly seems too loud,
and you have the uneasy feeling
the joke you'd thought was perfect
might not be
so funny after all.

I hesitated,
as if saying Nick's name out loud
would make my feelings real,
exposing my *xin*,
my *heart and mind*,
and I didn't want . . . what?

For my friends to laugh at Nick?
Or at me for choosing him?
Neither of these worries
seemed to be quite true
so I pushed aside my doubts
and told them his name.

Liz raised her eyebrows
and said with a shrug,
"He's not bad."

"Oh, he's better than *not bad*,"
Nina said, nodding slowly
and flashing me a mischievous smile.

• • •

But my friends' approval
didn't quite dispel
the lingering feeling,
like being at the party
and going ahead with your joke.
You're talking too fast,
tripping over your words,
and as you rush to finish,
you realize
you've forgotten
the punch line.

UNEASINESS

Friday night after Baba, Mama, and I
came home from the restaurant,
I sat at my desk sketching tigers.
Try as I might
to capture their forms,
nothing I drew seemed to look
quite right on the page.

I ran a fingertip along a tiger's spine,
feeling a thinness to the paper
from so much erasing,
when suddenly
the uneasy feeling returned,
after trailing behind me all day

like a small dog
snapping at my heels.

Now it threatened
to overtake me, bearing down
with a threatening growl.
This time instead
of trying to escape,
I looked straight at it until
it backed away a few paces
and snapped at me with its teeth;
still I didn't look away,
I stared it down until
the source of the feeling
grew clear.

GYM CLASS

The first time we changed into gym suits
for eighth grade P.E.,
the girls' dressing room
was dizzy with chatter,
the air sharp with hair spray,
aerosol sweet. Baby powder
puffed out in floury clouds,
making me sneeze.
"Sorry." A girl named Michelle
looked up and smiled,

then went back to silking powder
into her skin.

Talc shone
over the curves
of her sun-tanned shoulders and chest,
making them glow hickory-rich
against the snowy cotton
of her bra. She
pulled on her gym shirt
and I looked away,
self-consciously hunching
my own pale shoulders
and skinny chest.

Just then,
Squeeeeeeeeeee
of the gym teacher's whistle; and
trailing floral and musk scents
in our wake, we
thronged out into the gym,
our limbs flashing vaguely green
under fluorescent lights,
our tennis shoes squeaking,
shrieking against the floor,
echoing through
the sweat-rank
mildew-dank
disinfectant tang
of the gym.

. . .

Then, from the other
dressing room, a rumble,
growing thunder, stampede
of running feet, rubber soles
chirp-burping, sneakers
pounding down,
slamming hard
as the boys
stormed out
into the gym. Sweet,
high notes of cologne,
deodorant, mousse
rising above the smells

of sweat and boys' skin.
"Hey, Michelle," a boy
called out, followed by
a wolf whistle
that pierced
the cavernous gym
and echoed back
sexy and sly.

A couple of boys
guffawed, a girl
giggled, and the gym teacher
bellowed, "Settle down!"
Echoes of her voice
came back to us
watery and distorted

as her stern look
swept over us.
I sneaked a look
at Michelle,
who stared straight ahead,
with eyes bright and cheeks flushed,
and I wondered
what it might be like
to have a boy
whistle like that
at me.

"Listen up for your names!"
As the gym teacher called roll,
we answered, echoes
of our voices rubbery-loud
as they bounced
and overlapped.

Nearly through
with the alphabet
when she said, "West!"
and a voice
across the gym answered,
"Here."

The boy
who spoke
shook his hair from his face

then looked over
in my direction
and smiled.
He was so
good-looking
the teacher had to
call me twice:
"Wu . . . Emily Wu!"
"Here," I said
and the boy turned
and looked
right
at me.

For a moment
I gazed back,
noticing
the light freckles high
on his cheekbones.
I was trying
to make out the color
of his eyes,
when he swallowed
his lower lip
in an exaggerated overbite,
put his palms together
in mock-prayer,
stretched his lips thin
in a grin, squinted

his eyes into slits, then
jerked his head toward me
and said, "Ah-so!"

Quickly,
I turned my head,
breathless
as if I'd taken
a punch
in the gut.
But before
I looked away
I saw that his eyes
were blue.

LONGING

Sitting in the geometry classroom
in the minutes before class started
on a Friday morning in October,
I looked out the classroom window
to see a spattering of rain on the glass
and a gray haze cloaking the air.
I yawned,
chafing against
the closed, musty feeling of the room.

A shriek and a chorus of giggles

made me look up,
and through the classroom doorway
I saw a group of freshman girls rush by.
I was about to look away
when someone else came into view.

It was a boy who'd stopped
to talk to someone.
His back was to the doorway,
so I couldn't see his face,
but there was something familiar
about his blue jacket
and the way he stood easily,
with back straight
and his stance relaxed.

Just then,
he glanced into the classroom,
and I recognized
the new junior,
Nick.
Color rose to my face
and I wondered
if I should smile at him.

But the moment passed
as he glanced away,
then disappeared from view.

• • •

The room seemed suddenly to lighten
and I looked back at the window.
I saw the sun fighting
to break through the clouds,
and in the quicksilver light,
hovering
between brightness
and gray,
I felt an aching,
a powerful longing
for something
I couldn't name.

Home from the Restaurant 75 ⟶

It was nearly 11 p.m.
when Baba, Mama, and I came home
from the restaurant this Sunday evening.

Usually I only worked weekends—
most Friday and Saturday evenings,
but my parents would let me take a night off
to do something special with my friends.

Tonight we were short-staffed;
our chef had unexpectedly quit
and a waitress called in sick.
At first when I'd offered to work,

Baba shook his head,
and Mama said, "No, Emily . . ."
before I could even finish my sentence.
But when I reminded them tomorrow
was a teachers' work day
and I wouldn't have school,
they agreed I could help tonight.

I'd planned to work on
my sketches for the mural
when we got home.
But as soon as I headed upstairs,
I collapsed onto my bed.
My head still rang with restaurant sounds,
the clamor of the exhaust fan,
the clanging of the spatula,
the hissing of vegetables in the wok.
Now I didn't want to get up,
not even for pencil and paper.
I buried my face in my pillow
and closed my eyes.

After resting a bit,
I wanted a shower
to wash away the smells
of cooking oil, fried food
and cigarette smoke
still heavy on my hair and clothes.
I imagined the spray of water

coursing over my shoulders and face
and felt suddenly thirsty.
I headed downstairs
to the kitchen for a drink.

As I approached the kitchen
I saw Baba and Mama
were already there.
Baba sat at the table
reading the newspaper,
while Mama leaned back in her chair,
her eyes closed as she soaked
her feet in a basin of water.

Just then, the tea kettle
began to whistle.
Mama startled
then straightened in her chair
as if to rise.
Baba looked over at Mama,
he waved his hand at her,
urging her to stay seated
as he said, *"Ni zuo ba, wo lai,"*
You sit, I'll get it.

Mama smiled and sank back
into her chair
while Baba poured
two cups of chrysanthemum tea,

its flower and herb scent
drifting to the doorway
where I stood.

As I watched, Baba placed
one cup before Mama
and another at his own seat.
"Lai he cha," he said to Mama.
Have some tea.

Mama opened her eyes
and smiled her thanks.
She reached for the towel
draped over the arm of her chair,
but Baba got to it first.

He opened the towel,
then knelt before Mama's chair.
He dried first one foot
and then the other,
his touch so careful
as he patted away the water,
I found myself looking away.

Neither of my parents had noticed me
standing in the shadows
just beyond the doorway,
so I turned and made my way
quietly back up the stairs.

SEEDS

Before I began to sketch the tiger
I imagined him walking
through tall grass,
padding silently on great soft paws,
his fiery flanks waving
the grass as he passes
so it rustles and sways
as if from a sudden breeze.

I drew the grass, strands rising up
supple and high from the soil
where they began as seeds,
fine light grains
blown and scattered by wind,
then falling down
to rich dark earth.

I wondered what it might be like
to lie curled in the hull,
snug within
the comfortable dark,
sleeping warmly
the long night through
until points of sun filter in,
bringing heat and light
and the scent of the air above.
Next the seed feels

a welcome wetness,
she finds herself floating down,
swirling and sinking
into rain-softened soil
where she's blanketed deep
in the loamy black.

What powerful instinct
drives the green spark
to come bursting forth
with a push so mighty
she splits the skin
of her home,
even with the knowledge
she'll never return
to its safe sweet warmth?
What sense is it that pulls her
away from everything she's known,
urging her instead
to lift toward the sun
a slender sprout
aspiring to grow
and later perhaps
to bloom?

MAKEOVER

At school on Halloween day,
we were sitting at our usual lunch table
when Nina asked, "Do you remember
your first Halloween costume?"

"I dressed up as a cat," I said,
remembering the costume Mama had sewn me.
It was cut from a fabric so furry and soft,
I took the costume to bed with me
when she finished it.
That Halloween, Mama used an eye pencil
to draw whiskers over my cheeks,
and on my nose she dabbed
a triangle of pink lipstick.
When I looked in the mirror
and saw the cat peering back,
I felt graceful and strong,
as if I could leap
and twist in the air,
my spirits as bright
as the autumn leaves outside.

"That must have been a cute costume,"
Nina said now, smiling.
She sighed and added, "Don't you wish
we could go trick-or-treating tonight?"

• • •

I smiled. "That would be fun."

"Wouldn't it?" Liz agreed.
"I always loved dressing up.
My first costume was my favorite, ever.
I was a princess."
She smiled at the memory. "That was the first time
I ever wore makeup. I felt so glamorous."
She thought for a moment, then said,
"I know! You guys can come over today,
and we'll give each other makeovers."

When Nina and I went to Liz's house after school,
I didn't plan on getting myself made over,

but Nina said she'd found
the perfect lipstick for me.
Liz offered to do my hair
and when I hesitated, she said,
"Come on, Emily. Live a little."

I still wasn't sure
but Nina met my eye
and gave me a bright smile,
saying, "What could it hurt to give it a try?"
She was right, I decided,
it couldn't hurt to try, could it?

So Liz coiled my hair in a French twist,
combing, pulling, and twisting the strands

until my scalp went tingly and warm
and I felt like a cat being stroked,
languid and loose
as her fingers worked through my hair.

Then, facing Nina,
I felt a cool, steady pressure
as she rubbed lipstick onto my lips;
the tickle of eyeliner,
a fluttering touch
as she brushed mascara
onto my lashes
with a tiny black wand.
Finally she stood back,
looking pleased.
She handed me a mirror and said,
"What do you think?"

At first all I saw was
a Mouth,
large and red
like a target;
lips too big,
too bright,
too bold.
"It's way too much," I said,
reaching for a tissue.
"No, don't!" Nina said, grabbing my wrist,
"It's perfect."

. . .

Liz eyed me critically
for a long moment
and I raised my eyebrows, wondering
what she was thinking.
"You look very elegant," she said.
"If I didn't know better,
I'd think you were in college."
I was a little surprised
to hear such a compliment from Liz.

I must have caught something
of my friends' enthusiasm,
for the more I looked,
the more I came to like
the look of the girl I saw
in the mirror.
Maybe it was the fun
of being fussed over
or the excitement
of a new look;
but with my eyes
lined kohl-black,
I felt like Bast herself,
the Egyptian cat goddess,
queenly and sleek.
Lipstick dark
as ripe raspberries
made my mouth look

surprisingly mature
and knowing.

The girl
gazing out from the mirror
tilted her head back a bit.
She looked poised,
even mysterious
as she smiled;
it was as if she knew
a secret
you were dying
for her to share.

Tiger Sketch

At home in my room,
sketching a tiger for the mural,
I thought of our next-door neighbors'
tabby kitten.
Even in him, a distant cousin
of the jungle cats,
something tiger-like remained
in his cinnamon coat
striped boldly black,
and the gold of his eyes,
great light-gathering orbs,
the pupils shrinking to slits

in the brightness
of the afternoon sun.

Blinking lazily,
soaking in heat
as he lay on his side in the grass,
the tabby kitten
stretched out full-length,
extending his claws
from the tips of his paws,
flexing them luxuriously
through the air.
When I ran a hand over his fur,
it was hot to the touch,

gritty with dirt,
crackling with a static charge.
Suddenly, he leapt up
and playfully
batted at my hand,
then lightning-fast
he caught it,
trapping my hand
between his paws.
Baring his teeth
in a mock-snarl,
he dropped to his back
and buffeted me
with his strong rear feet
before spinning away,

leaving behind
pinpricks blooming red
where his tiny claws pierced
the skin of my wrist.
He sprinted across the grass
then stopped, twirled in the air
and landed lightly
on all four feet,
his eyes wild
his tail lashing
and the hair on his back
standing on end,
making him look
twice his usual size.

Later that day when he slept,
the tip of his tail twitched
and a low growl escaped
from his throat.
In his dreams was he
a tabby kitten no longer,
transformed instead
into a being
as grand and fierce
as his cousin,
the tiger?

NICK

On the Monday after Halloween,
I was caught in the rush
before lunch, borne along
with the press of bodies,
snatches of laughter
and talk, occasional yells,
smells of chewing gum
and hair spray, rubber
sneakers and sweat,
when suddenly
I saw
Nick
heading straight
toward
me.

He smiled at something,
blue eyes crinkling
at the corners,
a dimple flashing
at one side of
his mouth. He
looked toward me
and I ducked out
the side door,
moving so quickly
I tripped,
spilling my books outside.

• • •

Cheeks and hands stinging
with embarrassment
and cold, I was thankful
the November weather
kept everyone else inside.
I stooped for my books
when the door squeaked
behind me and
footsteps approached.
"Let me give you
a hand with that."

I looked up and my breath
puffed out clouds
of astonishment.
It was
him,
gathering my books.
"I'm Nick,"
he said with a smile
that made me dizzy.
"And you're . . . ?"
"Emily."
"Emily . . . ?"
"Wu."

A kernel of pleasure
was starting

to warm me
when he asked,
"Are you
Chi-nese,
Japa-nese,
or Vietna-mese?"
Something within
my stomach
clenched
and I felt as raw
and exposed
from the inside
as my face was
to the bitter air
outside.

Noticing my expression,
he raised both hands
palm-up,
as if in surrender.
He smiled
disarmingly
and said, "I thought
you might be Japanese
like my ex-girlfriend
at my old school."

In Chinese,
eating vinegar

means *feeling jealous*
and I tasted
a sharp sourness.
"My parents are
Chinese,"
I said,
wanting to be different
from this ex-girlfriend,
yet glad, somehow
to know he'd been interested
in an Asian girl.

This contrary set
of feelings
made me feel
as if I'd drunk down
two things that
didn't mix, like
soda pop and milk.
To distract him
and myself from
this queasiness,
I asked, "What's
your last name?"
"Hancock."

As he stood before me
smiling, his hair glinting gold
in the pale sunlight, so close

I could see the diagonal weave
of his checkered shirt,
a new feeling trembled
in my gut, delicious
as the way I used to feel on Christmas Eve,
unable to wait for morning.
I savored the knowledge
sweet as a secret
that *Nick*
stood outside, his nose
and the tips of his ears
reddening with cold
as he talked
with *me*.

As sudden as the winter breeze
that rose, making us both shiver
involuntarily and laugh,
a rush of daring surged,
warming me until
there was a buzzing
and humming inside,
and I heard myself say
in my best Cockney accent,
"Ni'olas 'ancock,
a fine name indeed."

Nick looked surprised
and I held my breath,

waiting.
Then he laughed,
sending out clouds
of breath into the frosty air
and my heart beat
fast with gladness.
"Do you want to go have lunch?" he asked.

Carrying his own books
and mine in one arm,
he held the door for me
with the other. My
cheeks and lips
tingled as warm
air touched
my skin, and
I nodded,
yes.

TIGER IN REPOSE

As I started another tiger sketch
I thought of Nick
and felt the stirrings
of heat from within,
the quickening of my heartbeat
rhythmic and insistent
as the pounding of drums

echoing through the foliage of
the tiger's jungle home.

The tiger
lies stretched on his side,
his stripes blending in
with the pattern of light and shadow
on the ground where he reclines.
The tip of his tail
twitches like a kitten's,
a willow-soft wand
lazily curling
then unfurling.
Even in repose

with eyes half-closed,
his whiskers stiffen
and the sleek cups of his ears
angle and turn
to track each sound—
the whisper of a leaf
falling to the ground,
the rustle of a twig from beneath
the claw of a quail.

The wind lifts, carrying
the smell of the quail
to the tiger.
He breathes in her scent
so warm and sweet,

but delicious sleep
also beckons.
He shifts where he lies
and his muscles
ripple over his flanks,
his flame-bright stripes
murmur and sigh
across his velvety skin.
Plenty of time yet
for the hunt to begin,
he thinks as he drifts
to sleep.

FLYING

When I'm in the world of a painting,
the air strong with the mix
of linseed oil and turpentine,
and busy with the scrape
of my brush against canvas,
I'm fixing the composition,
ordering the space,
navigating earth and sky, bird-like:
I stand back to see the painting from afar—
sighting the landscape,
then come in close for the tiniest details—
the sheen of a petal, fine hairs on a leaf;
it's the closest I think I'll ever come
to flying.

Painting the Tiger

Working on the mural after school,
I painted the tiger I sketched,
now awake and fully alert
as he crouched beneath
a banyan tree.
I touched crimson and gold,
yellow and orange
onto his lean sides
and powerful shoulders;
I added shadows to the muscles
waving beneath
his shining fur.

I started when a voice behind me
said, "Your tiger is very fierce."
It was Alex.
His next words
surprised me even more
when he gestured
to my tiger and said,
"If our football players
looked more like that,
maybe we'd be having
a better season."
After one surprised moment
I laughed.
Alex smiled back
and the sound of our laughter

echoed through
the hallway outside.

Before English Class

Nina, Liz, and I took our usual seats
in the English classroom
a few minutes before class started.
Amid the general chatter,
Nina turned to me and asked,
"Did you tell Nick you could go
to the mall with him this weekend?"

At her teasing smile
and the mention of Nick,
I felt my face flush and I nodded. "Yeah."

Nina grinned and said,
"So it's official. You and Liz
are both dating juniors."
She turned to Liz and said,
"Marshall must know Nick,
since they're in the same grade."

Liz hesitated then said,
"Well, Marshall says Nick
isn't in any of his classes."
To me she added, "I suppose

it might be hard for a transfer student
to get placed in the advanced classes
once the school year's started."

But the dubious look on her face
and her superior tone of voice
belied her words.
Liz looked as smug
as the child at a party
who held the prettiest balloon.
I tried to think of a retort,
one sharp enough to deflate her,
but all I could imagine
was a fancy silver balloon

bobbing just out of reach.

Just then, Nina touched my hand
and said, "Did I tell you Nick
always says *hi* to me
when he passes me in the halls?
Even though I'm only a lowly sophomore.
I think he knows I'm your friend."
She gave me a warm smile and said,
"He seems so nice, Emily."

I managed a small smile back at her
just as the bell rang,
signaling the start of class.
As the room quieted

I tried to forget Liz's comment
and to think instead of Nick.
Remembering the way
he smiled when he saw me,
anticipating the touch
of his hand on my shoulder,
all traces of annoyance vanished.
I felt myself floating up high
like a balloon released to the sky,
drifting up toward the clouds
until it's nothing but a glint
of silver on blue.

Wash It Off

I knew I was taking a chance
by putting on lipstick before
I left for school that morning;
I knew I might run into Mama
before I could make it outside.
But perhaps a part of me
wanted to find out
just what would happen
if she did see me.

And sure enough, Mama saw me
with lipstick fresh on my mouth.
She looked startled at first, then alarmed,

the way you might feel
while watching a tragic movie
at the moment when danger threatens.
By the time the movie's nearly done
you feel sad, but not truly surprised.
You've known all along
the hero would die
while saving someone else,
or that the star-crossed lovers,
no matter how deserving,
would never stay together in the end.
But knowing all this doesn't stop you
from hoping for the best
all the same.
100   And it doesn't keep you
from feeling as though you could weep
for the way things turned out
in the end.

As Mama continued
to regard me,
a look of such sadness
came into her eyes
I wanted to fall to my knees
and hug her
the way I would do
when I was small—
burying my face in her softness,
breathing in her comforting

mother-scent,
I'd ask her
to forgive me.

When Mama saw
the remorse on my face,
her expression changed
to one I'd seen before.
It was the same look she'd turn
on a burned pot, grim but determined
as she soaked the charred metal
then took up the steel wool
to scrub and scrape away
every last bit
of the stubborn, scorched mess
until the pot gleamed
silver again.

"Wash it off," Mama said to me now.
Her voice was stern, chiding me
as if I were a child
caught doing something wrong.

But I wasn't a child anymore
and I started to argue.
"Mama . . ."

"Go," Mama said, cutting me off.
"Go wash your face."

• • •

Just then, I heard Nina's car outside,
She was giving me a ride to school.
I didn't want to make us late
so without another word
I went back inside the bathroom.
When I emerged
Mama inspected me.
Only when she saw
that every trace of lipstick
was gone from my lips
did she nod,
the way she would
once she was satisfied
her pot was spanking clean.

But once a pot has been burned
that badly
no amount of cleaning
can restore the coating
that was scorched away
and the pot
will almost certainly
burn again.

Tomorrow before school,
I resolved,
I'd hide the lipstick
inside my backpack

and put it on after
I left the house.

CHILL

Home from the restaurant Friday night,
I considered what to wear
for my date with Nick tomorrow.
It was Thanksgiving weekend,
almost a month since we'd met,
and we were spending as much time
together as we could.
I hadn't told Mama and Baba about Nick.
I told them I was working on a project for school,
so they said I could take the day off.

I changed into a red sweater,
then looked into the mirror.
My hair was shiny
and flat with static,
the strands crackling
as they brushed my shoulders.
The sweater made
my cheeks glow pink,
the flush deepening
as I thought of Nick.

I felt a shiver deep

in the pit of my stomach,
as though I were on a roller coaster,
feeling my body tilting back
and hearing the grinding of gears
as the car made its way
up the tallest hill.
There was a dizziness,
the loud pounding of my heart,
as I anticipated the moment of lightness,
the feeling of being suspended
in air before
the crazy downhill drop.

Suddenly, cutting through
my excitement,
a chill as if
from a sudden wind,
coldness seeping in
through the cracks,
hidden gaps you can't repair.

I tried to concentrate
on thoughts of Nick,
but I couldn't shake the feeling,
a skulking,
inescapable knowing
that something
I'd just as soon avoid
was waiting just ahead.

• • •

Turning away
from the mirror,
I pulled off the sweater.
I felt the scrape of wool against my cheeks
and caught a whiff of its lanolin smell,
creamy and comfortingly sweet.
Goose bumps prickled
my bare shoulders and arms,
and I hugged myself
against the chill.

I avoided looking back
at my reflection in the mirror,
but somehow I knew
there was no escaping
the wintry coolness within,
until I discovered
its source.
So I squinted into
the wind,
and with eyes watering
and teeth aching,
I stepped deep
into the cold.

THE SWEATER

I.

When I was in sixth grade,
Little Aunt sent me
a white wool sweater
from Taiwan.
It smelled vaguely
buttery
as I pulled it
over my head,
its rough nub
sending my hair
crackling, sticking
in crazy swirls
to my cheeks, strands
lift-dancing
above my head.
Rising up against
the snowy
loops of sweater,
scrawled across
my stomach and chest,
houses mauve
and gray, their
peaked roofs notched
in the way of knitted triangles,
the way children draw

Christmas trees:
de-*dum* de-*dum* de-*dum*
down the sides like
stair-steps.

Mama and I both thought
the sweater
would look best
with the peacock-
green pants
she had made me.
I remember
standing still,
very still
as the cloth
whispered
kitten-soft
against my leg,
the pads
of Mama's fingers
brushing
my skin
as I turned
in a slow circle
a little that way
again
again
while she
slid the pins

carefully through
generous cuffs,
before basting
each leg.
Then,
snick, snick
the lovely
sound of Mama's
sewing shears
cutting through thick
shimmery waves
of green-blue
cloth.

108   On a brisk November morning,
I pulled on the white
wool sweater, inhaling
its lanolin warm
scent and feeling
its prickly kiss
against my cheeks.
I stepped into the peacock-
green pants,
the fabric's nap furry
against my skin.
I slid my fingers
up and down
my green-blue thighs,
the cloth slippery

under my fingertips,
shining like satin,
making me feel
fancy as royalty.
Above the pants, my
new sweater
glowed,
luminous and white
like a pearl.

Once I was dressed,
Mama and I
stood looking
at my reflection.
I saw her face
in the mirror
smiling at me,
warming my cheeks
until I felt
a pinkening.
"Hao piao liang,"
Mama said. *How*
pretty.
I ducked
my head,
in the face
of such joy,
because at
that moment

I knew
she was right.

II.

As I thumped
down the steps
of the school bus
that morning
and headed toward
the junior high, I felt
a tingle
from the skin
of my face
to my scalp,
a flutter
like a bird
beating its wings
inside my chest,
a quickening
of my senses
as I joined the press of kids
thronging inside.

What noise,
shouted greetings
and shrieks, throb
of voices, jostle
of bodies, smell

of hair spray, musk
perfume above
the sourness
of sweat
and breath.

Then, through the din
I caught a couple of words
right behind me:
"White sweater."
Then louder, closer,
I heard, "Look at that girl."

The voices so near, I wondered
if they might mean me.
A little embarrassed
but pleased by the praise,
I straightened my shoulders
and glanced up to see who was talking.

Right behind me,
two girls in tight,
cropped shirts,
heads together, whispering.
I recognized them from homeroom,
but I didn't know their names.
They looked old enough
for high school
almost, with fair hair
shiny with hair spray,

slim noses, powdered cheeks,
lips glossy with color.

One of them looked up
and poked her friend.
"Shhh! She's looking."
With a quick glance at me,
they brushed past,
leaving behind
a perfumey smell,
a trail of giggles.

I was wondering what
those girls were saying

when suddenly, alarm-loud
a bell ripped through
the jabber of noise
and kids separated
into two opposite waves
of movement up
and down the halls.
Heart pounding, I drifted
with the swell of kids until
I reached my homeroom.
I walked into
a nearly full classroom.
So many staring faces,
I looked away and headed toward
an empty desk up front.

• • •

That's when I heard a girl saying
in a voice loud enough
for me to hear,
"Look at that
see-through sweater!"
I looked up to see
the girls from the hallway,
flashing smiles like knives
as they looked straight at me.

Head down, face flaming
I was almost at my seat
when the same girl said,
more loudly this time,
"Look! She's wearing
an *undershirt*!"
Through a numbness
like novocaine,
shrouding the pain
sure to surface later, I felt
my undershirt burning
until it blazed
white hot
from beneath
the sweater.

I tried to sit down quickly
but my foot slipped
and I fell

into the seat,
jamming my elbow
against the desk,
hitting the funny bone,
pain twanging up
as the laughter rose
around me like waves
of heat steaming up
or plain
naked
shame.

The Dress

Saturday afternoon,
strolling through the mall
with Nick.
Everything seemed brighter,
the lights shining
inside the stores,
the sprinkle of melody
and the thump of bass beats
from the music store,
the melted butter smell
from the theaters
mixed with the stink
of stale cigarette smoke,
the heady drift of perfume

as we walked into
the department store.

I noticed girls
noticing Nick,
watched them look
from him to me
and felt their envy, palpable
as the static electricity bursts
made by our shoes
scuffing against carpeted floor.
I walked taller, savoring
the weight
of his arm
around my shoulders,
the tingle of my skin
where his hand
brushed my arm.

When I caught a glimpse
of our reflection in a mirror,
I almost believed
the girl
beside Nick
could be pretty
since he'd chosen her.
He leaned down to point something out
and I smelled, faintly
the sweetness

of shampoo
and the scent
of his skin.
"Look," he said,
his breath warm
on my cheek.

It was a mannequin
clothed in a dress
bright with a tropical print,
the fabric cut low
to show stiff, white curves
of fake breasts,
the sarong skirt
falling open
to bare a slim,
plastic thigh.

"You'd look fantastic,"
Nick said, "wearing that."
Something about the dress
bothered me, but I couldn't
quite say what it was.
"I'm not sure it's my style," I said.
"You'd look exotic, Hawaiian
or Polynesian. Just try it on."
When I hesitated
he put his mouth
to my ear

and whispered, "Please."
He reached out
and touched the fabric
of the dress
so gently,
I shivered.
"Okay."
I lifted
the dress from the rack
and walked to the fitting room,
aware all the while
of his hand, warm
on the small of my back,
as we walked.

Kissed by Nick

When Nick puts his arms
around me,
I feel a tingling,
as if I were
a musical instrument tuning,
with pegs loosening
and strings tightening,
until my skin feels
supple
and taut,
shivering

in anticipation
of the notes
to play.

When his mouth
touches mine,
I feel a thrumming,
strings vibrating,
body resonating,
my whole self singing
as I'm kissed
by Nick.

MONKEY

Sketching in my room
I thought of the new dress
hanging in my closet—
a slip of silk
bright as desire
its texture soft
as the way my skin felt
after my bath,
radiating heat
and steamy
with fragrance.

I'd planned to draw

another tiger for the mural
but instead
a monkey appeared,
sitting on a branch
high up in a tree.
With almost human features
in a wild, furred face,
she looks up with dark bright eyes
innocent and knowing
as the gaze of a newborn babe.

Curiosity glints in her eyes
when she hears a stirring
through the trees below.
Peering down
through the leaves, she sees
a flash of orange and black,
bright and enticing
like a lily
or tropical fish.

She makes her way down
drawing nearer and nearer
until she's close enough
to reach out an inquisitive hand
and touch the blazing stripes
moving with a slow, easy rhythm
as the tiger walks through the trees
so his pattern of fire and night

appears to shrink
and then stretch across
his shining fur
so plush and tempting
to the touch.

The monkey feels
a stiffening of the hairs
along her neck and spine,
she shivers as she senses
the tiger has become
aware that she is near.
She knows that he
could turn toward her
with one quick motion
of his mighty paw
or his powerful jaws,
that it is already too late
for her to flee.

She knows she should shimmy
back up the tree
and swing herself away
through the leaves,
but just then the tiger
turns his great head
toward her
and she sees
herself reflected

in the gold of his eyes,
yellow and ochre,
amber and brown
and gleaming with
a fiery light.

TESTS AND PARENTS

Our geometry tests came back
the week after Thanksgiving break.
Even as I sat with my friends at lunch
I could still see my grade:
a negative image
like a spot of harsh light
that lingers on the back of your lids
even when you close your eyes,
C.

Worse than the grade
was knowing
I could have done better
if I'd studied,
instead of spending so much time
with Nick
the weekend before the test.

"A C isn't bad, Emily," Nina said consolingly.
• • •

Liz rolled her eyes and said, "What is this,
the first C ever
in the history of Emily Wu?"
Unlike me, Liz had a natural talent
for math and science,
so I assumed she'd done well on the test.

I was sure of it when she said,
"Don't feel bad, Emily. It was a difficult proof."
I thought I heard a slightly victorious note
in her voice, but I was too caught up
in anticipating my parents' reaction to my grade
to give it much thought just then.

"Are you okay, Emily?"
Nina was looking at me with concern.

I forced a smile and said, "I'm fine.
I just don't think my parents
will be too happy about my test."

"At least they care enough
to be angry about your grades," Nina said quietly.

I looked at her, surprised.
"Your parents care about you."

"They do," Nina said. "But these days
they're more wrapped up in other things."

• • •

Liz gave her a shrewd look and said,
"How are your parents doing?
Are they arguing a lot?"

Nina shrugged and said,
"No more than usual."

Liz and I exchanged looks.
I knew we were both remembering
Nina's birthday last month,
when we went to her house for dinner.
Nina's father hadn't made it back
until we were nearly through eating.
"You're late," Nina's mother said,
her voice thin as a rubber band
stretched between a slingshot's two prongs.

"Just in time for cake and presents,"
Nina's father said,
his voice too bright and too loud
in the hushed room.
He brandished a large plastic bag
from the local toy store,
and pulled out an enormous teddy bear.
He held it out to Nina and said,
"Happy birthday, Nina."

"Thanks, Dad," Nina said softly.
"Thanks for getting it for me."

• • •

"Jeff," Nina's mother said, the name exploding
from her mouth like an expletive.
"Nina's sixteen, not six.
That's a completely inappropriate gift for her."
Her next words shot out
harsh as bullets: "You'd know it
if you were home with us
every now and then
for a change."

Nina's father went quiet
as a stone.
Neither he nor her mother

spoke to each other
for the rest of the evening,
but only to Nina,
in voices straining
toward cheerfulness.

As soon as we could politely leave,
Liz and I took Nina out for ice cream.
She wouldn't talk about
what had happened with her parents.
Today was the first time lately
she'd even mentioned them.

"Nina," I began now, unsure
of quite what to say.

• • •

"Everything's fine," she said,
cutting me short. "Don't worry."

Just then the bell rang,
signaling the end of lunch.
Nina busied herself arranging
her silverware neatly on her tray,
then gave me an apologetic half-smile.
"Try not to worry too much
about your test," she said.

She flashed me her usual, mischievous smile
and added, "Think about your weekend
with Nick instead. And don't try to tell us
the time you spent with him
wasn't worth one C."

Without waiting for my response,
Nina walked quickly toward
the kitchen with her tray.

I watched her retreating form,
feeling helpless
and wishing
I could have thought of something
reassuring to say to her.
Liz watched her, too,
then she looked back at me
and shook her head.

• • •

"I used to think Nina was lucky," she said,
"to have parents who were too busy
to pay much attention to her grades."
She smiled wryly.

I was quiet for a moment
before I nodded and said,
"I know what you mean."

Liz reached out her hand
for my empty lunch bag.
As I passed it to her,
our eyes met and I smiled.

Liz smiled back,
before taking both our trash bags away.
I waited for my friends to return
so the three of us could walk
together to class.

On the Way Home

Riding home on the bus
that afternoon,
I couldn't stop
thinking about my test.
As much as I appreciated
my friends' efforts

to make me feel better,
I didn't know if
they truly understood.
And I didn't really know how to explain
to them or anyone else
why my grades matter
as much as they do
to Mama and Baba.

Liz's mom works as a paralegal
for the firm where her dad practices law.
Both Nina's parents are engineers
at one of the local chemical companies
where Baba couldn't find work
in the days before he opened the restaurant.

Baba came to America on a student visa
for engineering graduate school.
When he finished his PhD,
he accepted a job teaching
at the community college.
But the pay was low, barely enough
to rent a nearby apartment
just big enough for Mama and him.
When Mama found out
she was pregnant with me,
Baba wanted to buy a house
for our family to live in,
a house in a good school district.

The three chemical companies in town
were hiring engineers at the time.
Baba submitted applications
for each of the positions
but he was never offered a job.
As Mama's time to deliver me neared
he finally decided
to open the Golden Palace.

For over sixteen years now
Baba and Mama have worked there
staying late every night,
seven days a week,
without weekends

or holidays
or paid vacation time.
I know that they *chi ku*,
that they willingly *eat this bitterness*
because they want
something better
for me.

SIGNING THE TEST

When I brought the geometry test
home to be signed,
Mama looked it over and said,
"What happened, Emily?"

She looked searchingly at my face
inspecting it for clues,
making me think of
the expression she wore
at the market choosing apples.
She'd check each one
to make sure it was firm
without any soft spots
to signal the presence of a bruise,
a flaw in an otherwise
smooth red apple,
its ruby skin striated
brick, gold, yellow, red,
light glossing over its curves
as she looked it up and down.   129 ⌒

Just then the expression
on Mama's face changed
as though she'd bitten into an apple
and tasted mush,
softening flesh beginning to spoil,
the beginnings of a bruise
she must have missed.
With the slightest twist
of her lips,
a shake of her head,
Mama said to me now,
"You can do better, Emily."
She handed the test back and said,
"Show Baba."

. . .

Baba looked it over
then without a word
he gathered fresh paper
and sharpened a pencil,
turning the handle of the upright sharpener
with a grinding of metal
gears against wood,
the harsh sound
echoing through
the quiet of our house.
A sharp *snap*
as the pencil lead
broke in the sharpener,
130   Baba expelled his breath
in annoyance or frustration.
He removed the pencil from the sharpener,
examined the broken lead,
rotated the pencil just so,
then put it back it into the sharpener,
turning the handle once more
until the pencil emerged
with a perfect point.

Baba worked through each proof I missed,
going step by step, filling the paper
with neat rows of letters and symbols,
his explanations methodical and clear
as if he were teaching a class.
"Now," Baba said when he finished,

"do you have any questions?"
I shook my head;
The problems I missed
weren't so difficult
I couldn't have gotten them right
if I'd studied.

"Next time," Baba said
in a mild voice free of reproach,
"If there's anything
you don't understand, just ask me."
I nodded, unable
to meet his eyes.
It was better for Baba to think
I hadn't understood
than for him to know
I hadn't done my best.

Baba picked up a pen
and with a single gesture
he signed his name, *Cheng-Wen Wu,*
the C written with one firm stroke,
the peaks of the Ws rising tall and proud
as a ship's masts, the sails full-blown.
It was the signature of a man
who wore his dignity easily,
whether dressed in a suit
for a formal event
or a spattered cooking apron

in the kitchen.
This was the worst part:
seeing Baba write
his name above my own
on a test paper
weeping
with errors.

CONFIDING IN ALEX

When I went to work
on the mural the next day
Alex was already there.

He looked up from the painting
with a smile of greeting
then studied me for a moment
and asked, "Is something wrong?"
I found myself telling him
about the test
and he nodded sympathetically.
"No one wants to disappoint
their parents," he said.
He thought for a moment, then said,
"You've done well
on the other math tests, haven't you?"
I nodded and he said,
"The semester's not over yet.
I think you can still make up for this one."

His smile was so kind
I found myself smiling back.

Just then, I noticed
what Alex was painting,
a group of ferns,
the fronds curling at the tips
like peacock feathers,
their thin-fingered leaves
ranging in shade
from brilliant blue-green
to cool slate-gray,
the color of the sky just before
it releases a gentle spring rain.
"What do you think?" Alex asked.   133 ⁓

"It's perfect," I said,
meaning it.
I picked up a brush
and when I started to paint
I felt something like calm
settling over me
like the mist that follows
a shower in May,
the wet air diffusing
the warm yellow sun
shining through.
Sometimes
on a day like this

if you're lucky enough,
you might even see
a fragment of rainbow
spreading itself
across the sky.

MASCARA

Morning minutes spent
in the bathroom at school,
stroking the curved
plastic wand
from base to tips
of my lashes.
I imagined my eyelashes
thick and long, dramatic
like the eyes of the model
smiling up from magazine pages
rich with perfume.

But on my eyelashes,
thin and short as eraser dust bits,
mascara lumped and clumped,
sticking and clinging
in tar-black flecks
and clots.
I considered my reflection
and sighed,

braced myself
for another try.

Stainless steel gleamed
beneath the long fluorescent bulb
above the mirror
as the silver jaws
of the eyelash curler
yawned.
My eye teared,
watery with the effort
not to blink
as the rubber-padded
metal instrument
loomed
large.

Sticky
crunch
of the two pads
chomping down
on my lashes,
gummy lift
of rubber pulling
away from
glop-wet
lashes. I
angled my head
to one side,

peering at
my lashes, dark-
lumped and slightly
bent.

Determined
to press on, I opened
my second eye
wide.
Glint of the
curler's approach
as I squeezed
on the handles,
jaws opening
up, then closing
down, brushing
against my lashes,
then suddenly
pain
smarting
white
I
let go
of the curler; I'd
accidentally caught
the lip
of my lid.

Blinking hard,

fluttering my eyelid
against the wash
of tears,
I stared down
through the wet blur
at the curler.
When the pain
went down
and my vision
cleared, I saw
(through one clear
eye, the other
rabbity pink)
the blurred
imprints of
my darkened lashes
on each of the curler's
rubber pads, two
feathery gray arcs,
faintly sticky,
shadowy
and quick
like the desperate
wing prints
of a startled bird
before it flew
away.

DINNER WITH NICK'S PARENTS

I.

A few days before Christmas,
Nick's parents invited me
for dinner at their house.
I hadn't told Baba and Mama I was going,
and I planned to be home
before they came back from the restaurant.

"Nicholas tells us
you're a very good student,"
his mother said,

placing her fork
on her empty salad plate
with a little *plink*.

"Oh no, I'm not
that good," I demurred
automatically.

"I'm sure you are,"
she said, smiling brightly.

"No, I'm not," I said again,
and Nick's mom
shot his dad
a puzzled look.

Ice clinked in my glass
as I took a sip of water,
trying to cool the heat
in my cheeks. Don't
be so modest, so
Chinese, I told myself.

Tomato sauce shone
slippery and red
over the chicken breast
looming large
on my plate.
Gently I eased
the tines of my fork
into the meat
and poised my knife.

Ringing *thunk* of my knife
skidding off meat,
hitting hard against
ceramic plate
as the chicken
slid free
and a fine spray
of orange-red sauce
dotted the snowy tablecloth.
Nick's mother jumped
a little at the noise, then
carefully
looked away.

. . .

My face was burning
when Nick's father asked
conversationally, "Do you know
Japanese, Emily?"

"No, I . . ."

"Dad," Nick broke in,
"Emily's *Chi*-nese, not
Jap-anese."

"I'm American,"
I said, but my voice
came out a mumble
and I don't think
anyone heard.

"We used to have Japanese
neighbors," Nick's father said,
smiling and looking at me
expectantly.

I was trying
to think of a response
when his mother added,
beaming, "They were just
the nicest family."

I forced a smile

in return, smiling
so hard
my jaws ached
and my cheeks
felt ready
to pop.

"Mom," Nick said, "Did I tell you
Emily's a great cook,
just like you?"

Nick's mom looked surprised,
as if she wasn't sure whether
she'd been given a compliment.
She smiled politely at me
and said, "Oh, yes.
Nicholas tells us your family runs
. . . is it a Chinese restaurant?"

"Yes."

"I love Chinese food," Nick's dad said heartily.
"Give me a couple of egg rolls and a plate
of chop suey
and I'm in hog heaven."

He smiled at me and said, "There's something
I want to ask you."

• • •

Something about the way
he was looking so intently at me
made me tense.
I felt brittle
as if the skin on my face
were as crinkly and thin
as an onion's outer wrap,
ready to slide off
at the slightest touch.
"Okay," I said.

"How would *you* say, 'chop suey'?"
Nick's dad asked.
"I want to know how to order it properly
in your language."

It was as though someone
had pulled
and the onion's outer skin
had slipped off,
revealing its next layer,
shiny white
and veined
with a delicate
network of green.
"I don't know," I said. "I think that's Cantonese,
and my family speaks Mandarin."

Nick's dad looked blankly at me. "All right.

How do you say 'fortune cookie' in Chinese then?
You must know that one."

Like chop suey, fortune cookies
don't exist in China.
"I'm not sure how to say that," I said.
But Nick's father looked as though
he didn't believe me,
so I explained, "It's not really a Chinese dessert."

"So why do they serve them at
every Chinese restaurant I've ever been to?"
Nick's father asked.

"I don't know," I said, unnerved
by the tremor in my voice.
"I guess people like to eat them," I finished,
hating the note of apology that crept into my tone.

In the silence that followed,
my skin prickled
as if I were an onion,
able somehow to sense
the sharp silver edge
of the knife
on the cutting board beside it.
"I've got it," Nick's dad said, snapping his fingers.

He gave Nick a sly smile and a wink,

then looked back at me.
"Tell us how to say,
'I love you' in Chinese."

My throat felt as tight
as the center of an onion,
packed in among smaller and smaller
layers of meat and skin.
I felt my face burning,
and I couldn't look at anyone,
not even Nick.

The waiting silence blared,
making my eardrums ring and my head ache.
Through the stinging waves
of embarrassment
rising from my face
the way vapors do
from an onion
that's been cut,
I managed to say,
"Wo ai ni." I love you.

Slowly and carefully, Nick's dad
pronounced, "Whoa heiney."
"Is that it?" he asked me.
I nodded, my gaze frozen
on the tiny lumps
of green pepper and onion

poking through the crimson
sauce on my plate.

"Whoa heiney," Nick's dad exclaimed,
his voice ringing out loud as a shot
in the quiet room.

Noticing
how precariously
my fork was balanced
at the edge of my plate,
I tried
to straighten it,
but my hand slipped
and the fork
fell onto the table,
its tines
staining the tablecloth
with a row of red dots
bright
as freshly drawn
blood.

II.

"They didn't like me."
My voice came out
unexpectedly harsh
and the words

hung suspended
in the cold air
inside the car.

Nick turned
the key in the ignition
and the engine
wheezed and gasped,
turning over and over uselessly
without catching.
He released the key
and in the sudden quiet
I wondered
whether he heard
the accusation
in my voice.

But when he answered
his voice was easy,
relaxed. "Sure, they liked you."
This time, the engine
caught, humming,
making the seat vibrate
beneath us. Air
blasted out from the vents,
blowing back my hair.
"My parents are cool,"
Nick assured me.
"They don't mind

when I date someone
a little
different."

I turned sharply
to stare at him,
feeling his words sting
like a handful of sharp pebbles
suddenly flung
into my face.
But Nick
just looked straight ahead,
oblivious, his handsome profile
impassive as a statue's.

The ride to my house
nearly over
and the word, *different,*
echoing through
the *haaaaaa*
of warm air blowing from the vents,
the monotonous song
of the turn signal
as we pulled into my driveway,
tires crunching over rocks.

The evening's uneasiness
settled in me
as heavily

as the undigested meat
in my stomach.

But then when Nick
turned off the car
and leaned toward me,
all unwanted feelings
disappeared
during the brief
sweet moment
he met me
for a good-night
kiss.

Noodle Soup

Steam rose from my bowl
of noodle soup, fragrant
with slivers of chicken and pork,
tangy with pickled cabbage.
The scent made me realize
how hungry I was and
I twined more noodles
around my chopsticks.
"Hao chi ma?" Mama asked,
concern in her voice.
"It's delicious," I assured her.
But she still looked

worried. "Did you argue
with Liz last night?"
I'd told Mama and Baba
I was having dinner with
Nina and Liz. I hadn't yet told them
Nick and I were dating.

Remembering last night's
dinner with Nick's parents
made the bitter
mix of feelings,
embarrassment, shame
and something else
I couldn't define
rise up in my throat
like bile.

"No," I said, "we didn't argue.
Everything's fine."
Mama was looking at me
like she knew there was more
I wasn't saying, so
I added, "I'm a little
worried about the
math test this week."
"You need to study more,"
Baba said. "If you study enough
you'll be prepared. Then
there's nothing to worry about."

Baba's refrain was familiar
but for once I was glad
to hear him say it.

Mama still didn't
look convinced,
so I smiled and said,
"The noodles are really good."
"No, they're not," Mama protested
but she looked pleased. "As
long as you like them."
"They're my favorite," I said
and Mama smiled.
"Don't worry about
the test. You'll do fine."
Suddenly I realized
Mama must have made this dish
especially for me
when she noticed
I was upset.

Steam from the soup
misted up, warming
my mouth and cheeks.
I heard an echo
of Nick's voice asking,
"So when do I get to meet
your parents?"

• • •

Just then, *shlrrr, shlrrr*
a loud slurp-sucking
interrupted the memory.
It was Baba, shoveling noodles
into his mouth with
his chopsticks, slurping
broth from his soup spoon
noisy as a child.
Mama puckered her lips
over her spoon
as if she were blowing
a kiss; she blew
delicately at the broth
before slurping gingerly,
lips vibrating loud
against the spoon, as she
sucked in liquid slowly
against the heat.

The sound of my parents
slurping their soup
was suddenly unbearable
and I blurted,
"Do you have to eat
like that?"

It was quiet
as Mama and Baba
both stopped eating and

looked straight at me.
The skin of my scalp
shivered, and I wished
I could take back the words.

"Hai yao ma? Have as much as you want,"
Mama said. "There's plenty."
My heart thumped loud
and fast in my ears
for a couple of beats
before I realized
they were eating too noisily
to hear me.

"Now isn't a good time
for you to meet them,"
I'd told Nick.
"Why not?"
"It's just not."
He didn't press me
and now, listening
to the dinner din,
I was glad he didn't.
I lifted a spoonful
of soup to my mouth,
the doughy flavor
of noodles, delicately
meaty, fresh with greens,
was so tantalizing,

yet comforting,
somehow, in its
familiarity.

Mama stood from the table
and walked over to the stove.
She lifted the lid of a pot
to stir its contents.
The metal spoon sang against
the sides of the pot as she stirred,
and the smells of soy sauce and aniseed
rose into the air.
I realized Mama was making
tea leaf eggs,
another of my favorites.

I felt a stab of guilt
at betraying
Mama and Baba with
my thoughts, disloyal
and mean.
I tried to lose myself
in the scent of spices and soy,
wafting pungent and sweet
through the kitchen. But
at that moment,
Baba slurped up
strands of noodles,
then burped
resoundingly.

• • •

The realization
sank down, heavy
and irretrievable
as a stone
thrown down
a well: I would never
invite Nick over for dinner
to meet my parents.

TEA LEAF EGGS

I was eight the first time
I helped Mama make *cha ye dan,*
tea leaf eggs.
We pebbled the shells
of the hard-boiled eggs,
carefully tap-tapping
as we turned them,
rapping them against
the counter until
the eggshells were cracked
all over, like
summer-dried earth,
the pieces webbed
together by the shell's
filmy inner membrane.

• • •

The crackly-shelled eggs
were ready for stewing
in Mama's deepest pot, the one
with fat handles on the sides
like pig ears.
Eggs ready for
her special brew
of jasmine tea leaves
boiled in hot water
with soy sauce,
a mixture of spices
and grapefruit pulp.

The tea leaves
were fragrant and light
in the palms of my two
cupped hands
as I sprinkled them into
the roiling water.
We dug
our fingers hard
into the tough, grainy
grapefruit skins,
rinds yellow and pebbly-smooth
on the outside,
spongy and milk-white
on the inside,
juicing the air tangy-sweet
as we split open

the clear, thin
skins of each
wine-pink
crescent wedge
of fruit.
We plucked out
the small
jewel-like strands
of pulp
and added
their bright
sharp
citrus tang
to the pot.

Finally, the eggs.
Mama let me hold
her long-handled spoon,
the weight of an egg
balanced at the center
of its shiny silver belly
as we drifted each egg down
through the hot steam
down into
the pungent
sweet
soy sauce
grapefruit
tea.

• • •

It wasn't until
the next day at school
that I saw the fresh tea egg
Mama had packed
in my lunch bag.
I unwrapped the plastic
swaddling the egg,
then began
to peel it.

Whisper of
the bit of eggshell,
delicate pull of thin
inner skin,
slight bite
of shell's edge
against
my finger
as I broke off the first piece
of sepia-brown shell.
I pushed my finger
against smooth
wet egg, lifting
free a spiral
of brown, cracked
eggshell
that slipped off
easily

in one
continuous
piece.

Clean as batik,
the egg was patterned
with fine brown
lines, as though inked
to show where
the cracks in its shell
had been.
The briny flavors
of soy sauce
and tea

in my nose,
I was ready to bite
into the egg
when I heard,
"Ewww, look! Look at what *she's* got
for lunch!"

It was Lisa,
the girl with the prettiest hair,
so light it was almost white,
shiny and soft like corn silk.
Lisa wrinkled her nose
and called out: "Look at that rotten egg.
You're not going to eat that
nasty egg, are you?"

• • •

My face got hot
and I glanced around
to see all those faces
watching me.
I scrunched the plastic wrap
back around my egg,
shells and all,
and crammed it back
into my bag.
"That Chinese egg
sure does stink," someone said,
I couldn't tell who.
"Rotten egg."

Then all the boys
and some of the girls
fanned their hands
in front of their noses.
"Something smells!
Rotten egg!"
I grabbed my lunch bag
and ran for the trash can,
where I threw
the whole thing
away
into the wide
sloppy,
stinking
mouth.

Passing Alex

The last day of school
before Christmas break, I was walking
to the cafeteria with my friends
when I saw Alex coming
in our direction.
As he approached,
one of his tennis shoes
squeaked
against the floor
and I noticed how bright and white
his shoes appeared,
fully exposed as they were
beneath the stiff round cuffs
of his blue jeans.

As we passed each other
he gave me a wave
and I waved back
quickly.
But Liz saw him
and she said, "One guy isn't
enough for you, Emily?"

I looked sharply at her
to see whether she might be
making fun of Alex,
but I couldn't quite read
her expression.

• • •

Just then I heard
another sharp squeak
from somewhere behind us.
I turned my head to see
Alex turning the corner.
Though he'd disappeared from view,
I could hear a series of shrill chirps,
like bursts of jeering laughter,
tracking Alex's progress
until finally,
mercifully they faded
from earshot.

I didn't dare look at Liz.
I felt a hand on my arm,
it was Nina. "Wasn't that Alex Huang,
your mural partner?"
I nodded and she continued,
"He's a really good artist.
The mural looks so amazing, Emily."

I thanked her
but I couldn't enjoy her praise.
I felt a slight chill
from within
as I wondered about
my own reaction to Alex.

• • •

When the two of us
painted together
I never noticed Alex's clothes
nor did I ever consider
how I might look to him,
wearing Baba's old shirt
as a smock.
I didn't know why I'd become
suddenly aware of his appearance
when other people were around,
or why I would feel
so bothered
at the thought of someone
making fun of him.

It was true that I felt
indignant on Alex's behalf,
but that was only a part of it.
As we reached the cafeteria,
smells of overcooked kale
and the greasiness of fried potatoes
made me feel slightly queasy
and I realized
I didn't want people to think
I was too much
like Alex.

Apple Drawing

As I sketched in my room that night,
my pencil felt clumsy and thick in my hand,
like the large, round pencil of a kindergartener
as she painstakingly learns how to write
each letter of the alphabet.
With their wooden faces and awkward limbs,
my monkeys seemed to mock me from the page.

Time for a break, I thought,
and I went down to the kitchen for a snack.
On the table I saw a bowl of fruit—
banana, apples, and pears—
and I remembered
the summer before fourth grade,
drawing the bowls of fruit
Mama set up in the kitchen,
Mama telling me to *look.*

I didn't understand what she meant
until one day
when I was up before anyone else,
in the kitchen, blue
with first morning light,
and I took an apple from the bowl
and *looked.*

I held the apple in my palm,

feeling its heaviness
the coolness of its skin,
I sniffed a clover freshness
from the valley at its stem,
touched the fruit's curving faces,
saw the way it flared out on top
and narrowed toward bottom
like a cow udder, molar tooth,
or human heart;
I set it back on the table
and studied the shadows
darkening the planes
that fell away from the light,
noticed the brightness

illuminating rises,
and then I started
to draw.

The kitchen was warming yellow
as I finished this drawing.
Mama came down to start breakfast
and I showed her.
Mama smiled and said,
"Hua de hao." Well done.
"I knew you could do it."
My heart beat fast
with excitement
and pride
as I raced to find Baba.

I pounded up the stairs
and held out my drawing
to him.

Baba took it carefully
with both hands,
brought it to the window
held it in the light
and said, "You drew this
yourself?"
When I heard
the wonder
the praise
in his voice
I felt
suddenly shy.
I nodded,
too full for words.
Baba's hand rested
on my head for a moment
and he said,
"This is very good,
Emily."

The spot
where his fingers touched my hair
stayed warm, somehow
as if I'd just come inside
from a day so bright

my hair was hot to the touch,
sun lighting the strands
plum-blue
coppery-red
a dark iridescence
reflecting
the radiance
of the day.

CAUGHT

Sunday afternoon
two weeks after Christmas break,

I'd told Baba and Mama I was meeting Liz
to work on a history project,
but the truth was
I didn't want to tell them
I had a date with Nick that day.
I thought Baba and Mama
had already left for the restaurant
so I came out of the bathroom
wearing makeup,
a snug shirt,
a short skirt,
and a pair of heels
I'd borrowed from Liz.
I don't know which of us
was more surprised,

Baba or I.
He looked at me
with eyes wide, astonished
as though the girl standing frozen before him,
her hand on the bathroom door
and one foot lifted mid-step,
wasn't his daughter of sixteen years
but someone he didn't know at all.

The look on his face reminded me
of the time, two years ago,
when we were driving home from the restaurant
and an elderly woman driving beside us
crossed over into our lane
and scraped the side of our car.

Before it happened
I'd watched through my window,
shrinking back from the glass
as her car drifted closer and closer.
Things happened so quickly
I didn't have a chance
to call out a warning to Baba as he drove.
Yet in the moment before the accident happened
time seemed to expand—
stretching out rubbery,
almost comically out of proportion
like the image on an inflating balloon,
time warping
like the strange, manic sound of a musical toy

just before its batteries die out.
I felt a shock of realization,
knowing we were about to collide,
knowing there was nothing I could do to stop it,
then the lightning quick
electric chill
of fear
just before we were hit.

In Baba's expression this morning
I saw the same bewilderment,
as though what he saw
before his very own eyes
was so unexpected
and unwanted,
undeniable nonetheless,
and he was helpless to do anything
but watch.

Baba didn't say anything to me
as I walked past him
down the hallway,
down the stairs,
and out the front door.
The January wind lifted,
sending a handful of dried leaves
into a swirl above the driveway.
I shivered as the cold cut across my face.
When the wind died away,

the leaves drifted down
as if exhausted, their edges
making small scraping sounds
as they touched down on asphalt.
I thought about how I'd looked at Baba
when I passed him on my way out,
but he hadn't looked back at me;
he walked right past me into the bathroom,
with shoulders drawn in slightly.
Baba is a full head taller than I,
but as I watched his receding form that morning
it seemed we were nearly the same height.
It was the first time
I could ever recall thinking
Baba didn't seem so tall.

Sharing the Mural

At first I didn't show Mama
my sketches for the mural
because they were so new and raw
like wet clay
you've only begun to shape,
your palms still stinging
from slapping and pounding down slabs of clay,
then kneading them smooth
again and again
until the air is fragrant
with the smell of damp earth.

. . .

And ever since the time,
a couple of months ago,
when Mama made me
take off the lipstick,
I just haven't felt like
sharing the mural with her
at all.

I was in my room studying
when Mama came in just now,
bringing my tiger sketches.
I didn't mean to leave them out,
I was working on them
downstairs this afternoon
when Nick called.
I went upstairs to talk on the phone
and I forgot to bring
the sketches up with me.

Holding them now
Mama smiled and said, "Emily,
your drawings have so much heart."
Even as I warmed to her praise,
I noticed in her voice
such pleasure, even excitement,
almost as though the drawings in her hands
were her own artwork
and not mine.

. . .

I knew Mama had more to say
but I didn't want to hear
her suggestions;
I wanted the mural to be
all my own.
So before Mama could say
anything more I said,
"Not now, Mama
I'm busy."
The words came out sharper
than intended; Mama
looked so surprised
and hurt
that I added, "Maybe later,
I'm studying for a math test now."

My voice must have sounded
apologetic,
even conciliatory,
for Mama brightened and said,
"*Hao*, go ahead and study.
We can talk tomorrow
about feeling the way the tiger moves.
Your tigers are well-proportioned,
their moods are wonderful,
but they're just a little bit stiff
in places. I think you want
more of a sense of motion."

• • •

I felt heat rising,
blood pounding in my head,
my anger pulsing
through the air.
I wanted to tell Mama
I didn't want her help
but before I could say anything else
she placed the sketches on my desk
then headed for the door.
"Hao hao nian shu." Study well,
Mama said with a smile
as she left my room.

Still angry,
I slammed my math book shut
so forcefully
and carelessly
it slid off my desk
and its hard spine clipped
my toe as it fell.

Worse than having to hear
Mama's advice for my drawings
was the realization,
throbbing like a new bruise,
that Mama
was probably right.

Alex's Parents

All day today at school
I thought about Mama
behaving as if
she owned me
and my artwork,
and the more I thought,
the madder I got.
When I went to work on the mural
Alex was already there,
but without saying anything more
than a terse *hello*,
I went to work
painting with fierce strokes,
my anger hazing
the jungle air
red then black,
painting burnt sienna clouds
that loomed heavy across
an apocalyptic sky.
I took a step or two back
from the canvas
and saw it was too dark,
overdone,
even sloppy.
Discouraged, I lowered my brush
so carelessly I splattered the mural.

"Rats," I muttered
wiping off stray paint drops
with the sleeve of my smock.

Alex stopped painting
and gave me a questioning look.
I blew out my breath and said,
"Do your parents ever drive you crazy?"

Alex smiled and said,
"Of course."
Somehow that was the last thing
I expected him to say,
and for a moment

all I could do
was look at him
in surprise.

Alex laughed at my expression.
His look of amusement
was sympathetic nonetheless,
so I told him about Mama
treating me like a child.
"Does your mother
do that, too?" I asked.

"Sometimes she does."
He thought for a moment

then added, "I think all mothers
must worry. Also
I'm a *parachute kid*."

"A what?"

Seeing my puzzled expression
he explained, "That means my parents
are working full-time in Taipei,
while I've been staying here with my uncle
during the school year."

"But I thought you moved here
with your parents?"

"No. My parents' jobs
in Maryland didn't work out,
so they decided to go back to Taiwan to work.
They wanted me to finish high school in the States
and brought me here to live with my uncle."

"You mean you've been living away
from your parents since then?"

"That's right. But they've been back once to visit,
and I'll see them again for Chinese New Year."
It was hard to imagine
living so much on your own.
It was one thing to wish

you could be free of your parents
and another thing entirely
to have it be true.
"That must be tough," I said.
"You must miss them."

"I do miss them."
Alex's face was grave
and a little sad.
I was wishing I hadn't
brought up this topic,
when he brightened and said,
"Chinese New Year is coming soon,
so I'll see them before long.

And as soon as school lets out I'll be going
back to Taipei for the summer."

"That's good," I said
and smiled.
Alex smiled back
and said, "Yes, it is."

Almost at the same time,
we picked up our brushes
and returned to the mural.
I blended the slightest bit of blue
into white paint
and worked this mixture
into the sky

giving it a sense
of depth and light
like a new morning
after a night of storms.

Taking Flight

There sits the monkey
looking up at the tiger,
the tiger stands still
as he gazes back
while the sun shines down
through a filigree of leaves,
lighting the dust motes
floating through space
so they glitter and shine
and it seems as if
the air itself
is shimmering.
For the moment
all is quiet—
the birds cease their singing
and the insects their chatter,
the leaves keep still
and even the trees
seem to hold
their breath
as they wait.

• • •

Then suddenly
the tiger snarls
breaking
the monkey's trance.
She startles
then scampers away
up the tree.
When safe in her perch
high up in the leaves,
she looks down
at the tiger
and scolds him.
She bares her teeth
and shakes a fist,
shrieking with fear
and relief.

With a rustle of leaves
and a graceful leap
to another tree,
the monkey swings
herself away,
disappearing deep
into the green.
Even after she's gone
her screams echo back
so raucous and wild
they startle
a flock of birds.

• • •

With a rush of feathers
and the strong swift beating
of wings pushing through the air,
the birds lift up—
so many white spirits
rising, spiraling
higher and higher above.

The Dance

Saturday night at the Valentine's dance,
rumble of the bass beat
in my gut, mixing with
the shivery sweetness
of dancing with Nick.
It was only between songs
that I felt tiny bites
into the skin of my shoulders
from the spaghetti straps
of the tropical print dress.

But then the music
began again, a slow song
filling the dim cafeteria.
The silky swing
of my skirt against
my thighs, the softness
of his shirt under

my fingers, the feel
of his hands
on my waist, solid
and warm, making
my stomach
do a funny, wet
flip inside.

After the dance,
inside the car
I let Nick
press me closer,
closer as he whispered,
"Emily, my pretty

Emily, *my*
geisha."

Much later,
alone in my bedroom,
I unzipped the dress
with a quick loud buzz,
like the sound of bees
roused from their nest.
I stepped out of the dress's folds,
the silk wilting
like a tired corsage,
and the words, *my geisha*
echoed back,
cutting through

the residual tingle
of being with Nick.
The bones of my head
suddenly ached
with a gritty giddiness
as if I'd been crunching
grains of sugar
in my teeth.

Even the blessedly hot
water shooting out
from the shower head,
beating down loud
against glass walls,
couldn't drown out
the words,
my geisha,
Emily,
my geisha.

Nor could
the water erase
traces
of Nick's
hands
on my
guilty
skin.

The Birds

Painting the birds,
I imagined each stroke of my brush
a sweep of strong wings
lifting me up
until I sailed with the wind,
riding the currents
into the blue of sky.

As the birds flew high
above the trees
did they look down through
the canopy of leaves
to see tiny figures below?
Tiger and monkey,
small colored spots
soon indistinguishable
in a palette of greens and browns,
a pointillist landscape
turned abstract painting
in this aerial scene
distilled to the essence
of color and form,
being and light.
Painting, I longed
for the power of flight,
wings cleaving the air
cleanly as wind
while I soared.

• • •

But as much as I tried
to push them away,
thoughts of Nick
and the dance
settled over me
heavy and dense
like a fog.

Wish though I might
to fly away
I knew that even
the swiftest of birds
would have to alight
at the close of day,
returning to earth
to roost.

I set my brush down
for a moment to rest,
suddenly tired.

I felt so heavy
I didn't see how
I could
possibly
fly.

AFTER THE DANCE

On Sunday afternoon,
Nick called. As I held the phone to my ear,
vibrations from his voice
tickled my skin.
But instead of feeling
a feathery excitement rising inside,
I felt drained,
and the phone in my hand
so heavy,
it required all my strength to hold.
I imagined a bird
huddled on its perch,
184   plumping its feathers against the wind.

Nick invited me to go for coffee.
I knew I could have
gone out and come back
before Baba and Mama
came home from the restaurant
but I told Nick
I wasn't feeling well.

There was a pause
and I wondered
whether he heard through the fib
to the sadness beneath,
and I knew

if he asked me what was wrong
we would talk
and I might then feel the stirring of wings
and a lifting of hope,
but when Nick broke the silence
he said, "Okay.
See you at school."
His voice sounded normal,
almost cheerful.
When he hung up,
the click of the phone
seemed surprisingly loud
even harsh
but still louder
was the silence
of the dead phone line
in my ear.

FLAMES

On Wednesday night
when Nick called me,
he invited me over to his house
on Saturday to study.
This weekend at the restaurant
we'd be short a waitress,
so I told him I had to work.
I didn't say

I'd much rather be with him
or try to schedule another date.

There was a silence
over the phone
before Nick finally said,
"Look, Emily. Are you trying
to tell me something?"

Yes, Nick, I am,
but I don't know exactly what it is
I want to say . . .
Unspoken, the words
whispered in my mind.
186   With the phone against my ear
humming with the inflections
of his voice, each note familiar
as a favorite song,
I could almost smell him nearby
and imagine the warmth
of his hand on my shoulder.
I didn't know how to express
the longing I felt,
glowing like embers
swelling red-hot
with the promise
of fire.
But there was
something else, too—

doubt, cool
as a pail of water.

"Emily?" Nick sounded
slightly irritated, and his tone
sparked something
inside me, sharp
as flint on steel.
I felt a surge of power,
a bright blue glow,
and a voice in my head rang out:
I am not your geisha, Nick.

"First you're sick, now you have to work,"
Nick was saying, ". . . and it's like
you're avoiding me at school.
What is this?
You think we shouldn't
see each other anymore?"

It was the annoyance,
the incredulous note in his voice,
that made the smoldering
heat inside me
ignite into fiery tongues,
leaping up orange,
flaming red.
"Yes, Nick," I said.
"That's exactly what I think."

• • •

But when I hung up the phone
I felt a chill
as if a sudden strong wind
had snuffed the fire out,
leaving behind
darkness,
cold and indifferent
as a starless
winter
night.

INVITATION

At lunch the next day,
Liz told us she'd been accepted
to the local community college's
summer math program.

"Hey, Liz, that's great!" Nina said.

I knew Liz had worked hard
on her application,
and I was glad for her, too.
But my voice came out quiet
and strangely flat when I said,
"Congratulations."

• • •

Both Nina and Liz
gave me a questioning look
and I blurted out,
"Nick and I broke up."

Nina put her arm around my shoulders
and gave me a squeeze.
"Oh, Emily," she said, "I'm sorry."
She was looking at me
with such sympathy
that my nose stung
and tears threatened,
but I didn't want to cry,
so I looked at Liz.

I knew she didn't think
much of Nick,
and I was expecting
a dismissive comment,
even a disparaging one,
and I hoped her words
might even help
to distract me
from my misery.

But Liz only said, "I'm sorry
about Nick, Emily. I can imagine
myself in your shoes.
I know I'd be a mess

if Marshall and I broke up."
She spoke quietly
and with such sincerity
I did cry then.

Nina dug in her purse
for a tissue for me,
and Liz said, "Listen, why don't you guys
sleep over at my house on Saturday?
Do you think your parents will let you, Emily?"

"They might let me leave the restaurant
a little early that night.
And if not,
I can come after I finish everything."

"Then it's settled," Liz said.
"Nina can bake us her famous brownies,
and I'll supply the ice cream."

"I'll bring . . ." I began.

"You'll bring nothing," Liz said briskly.
In the same authoritative tone
she added, "This will be
a Feel-Better-Emily party,
and you're the guest of honor."

When I started to protest,

she softened her tone and said,
"Really, Emily. Just come
and have a good time
with us, okay?"

Nina gave me a smile
and nodded her agreement.
Everything went blurry and wet
as I said shakily
through a fresh wash of tears,
"Thanks, you guys. Thanks a lot."

News

Saturday morning, I came downstairs
for breakfast with Baba and Mama.
Mama lifted the lid of the bamboo steamer,
freeing a cloud of steam,
meat and vegetable smells wafting up
from the tender white buns inside.

The sun was streaming
through the kitchen window,
it winked off the tines of my fork,
making them burn
a deep silver in my hand.
I closed my eyes for a moment
against such brightness,

then suddenly
out of nowhere
I felt the ghost of a touch,
a flicker of silk
against my skin.
I wanted to keep
the feeling, to hold
it a moment longer,
but it vanished
like a dragonfly
glinting for an instant
in a rush of color
and then gone.

192 Baba's voice pulled me
out of my thoughts.
"Don't you want to hear
the good news, Emily?"
He sounded so pleased I wondered
what this news might be.

Mama was smiling, too.
"Do you remember," she said,
"the Chinese class your cousin Sophia
took in Taiwan last summer
and how well she spoke Chinese
when she came back?"

When I nodded she said, "We've worked it out

with my youngest sister,
your Little Aunt;
you'll be staying with her in Taipei
when you go there this summer
to learn Chinese."

I was so surprised to hear this
I said the first thing that came to mind,
"But I already know Chinese."

"You don't speak it with us," Mama said.

"We talk to you in Chinese," Baba added,
"but you answer in English."

Taiwan.
As I thought of the way
Mama and Baba had planned my summer
without even checking with me,
I felt a twinge of anger,
but strangely muted,
like moth wings fluttering at night—
a soft, powdery whiteness
as the moth makes her way toward a light.

As Baba and Mama looked expectantly at me,
I remembered the mural.
"I have to finish the mural this summer," I said.
"Mrs. Burns and Alex are counting on me."

When I'd told Mrs. Burns I might need
more time to work on my part of it,
she said it wouldn't be a problem
to finish over the summer.

"You'll only be gone during June and July,"
Mama said. "That should leave you
plenty of time to finish it up in August."

I didn't say anything else to Baba and Mama;
I didn't have the energy to argue.
I found myself not caring
whether or not I went to Taiwan
for the summer.

It was as though all my feelings
were extinguished,
like a moth brushing too close
to the light,
and quietly, unwittingly
snuffing herself out
in a flare of powder and smoke.

Even the thought
of being away from the mural
failed to move me.
I hadn't worked on it since
I painted the birds
after the dance with Nick.
Thinking of the mural now,

imagining the expanse of canvas,
bright with colors
and so full of life,
I felt a twinge as if from pain
and with an effort
I pushed its image
from my mind.

Mama and Baba were studying my face.
Perhaps they noticed my lack
of excitement at their news,
Mama gave Baba a quick look
and he said, "Don't worry
about the restaurant.
As you know, we have
a full summer staff.
We can manage without you
for a couple of months."
He gave me a smile and added,
"Besides, you deserve a break."

For his and Mama's sake,
I managed a smile.
Seeing the pleased looks
on their faces
I wished I could feel
a fraction of their pleasure,
but I felt nothing more
than a butterfly
pinned to a board

and encased in glass,
the colors of its frozen wings
bright as ever they were
when the butterfly
was still
alive.

SLEEPOVER

The thick metal handle
of the ice cream scoop was cool
and comfortingly heavy in my hand
as I dug deeply into
a carton of vanilla ice cream.
Liz was beside me
and Nina sat across the table from us
as we gathered in the kitchen
at Liz's house on Saturday night.
"I have more news for you guys," I said.
"I'll be spending most of the summer in Taiwan."

In answer to the surprised looks
on my friends' faces,
I said, "My parents arranged for me
to stay with my aunt there.
They want me to work on my Chinese."

"Wow!" Liz smiled broadly at me.
"I'm so jealous."

• • •

I smiled back. "No you're not.
You'll be too busy at math camp
to even think of me."
I was shaking ice cream
onto my brownie when Nina
dropped her spoon
back onto her plate so loudly
I looked up, startled.

I saw a mound of ice cream
slide off Nina's plate
and onto the table.
"I'm really sorry, Liz."
Nina sounded so upset,
Liz's eyes widened in surprise.

"It's *okay*, Nina," Liz said.
"No big deal."

Nina's hand shook
as she tried to spoon the ice cream
back onto her plate.
When it slipped from her spoon
and fell onto the table again,
she burst into tears.

"Nina?" I said, worried.

Nina was clutching her spoon so tightly

her knuckles went white.
"What am I going to do this summer
with both you and Liz gone?"

I saw my own shock mirrored on Liz's face.
"Nina!" she said. "I never thought . . ."
Her voice trailed off and she gave me
a helpless look.

"Neither did I," I said quietly.

"How are things with your parents?" Liz asked.

"The same," Nina said,
wiping the tears from her face.
Still holding the spoon,
she traced milky patterns
on the edge of her plate.
Her voice was calmer as she said,
"They both work such long hours,
I almost never see them.
And when they are home, they fight.
Then Mom goes into the den and turns on the TV,
Dad goes into the study and turns on
the computer, and it's almost like
they're not there at all."
She put the spoon down on her plate
with a little tinkling sound.
"And now, with both you guys
gone for the summer . . ."

• • •

I walked around the table to Nina's side
and put my arms around her.
"I'm so sorry, Nina."

"I'm sorry, too, Nina," Liz said, joining us
and hugging her, too.

Nina hugged us back, then took a deep breath.
She gave us a watery smile and said,
"It'll be all right.
Maybe I'll try to find a part-time job or something.
I'll need the money anyway to buy stamps
for all the letters I'll be sending you guys."

It wasn't until much later that night,
when we were in our sleeping bags in Liz's room
and I thought both Nina and Liz
had fallen asleep,
that I heard Liz's voice whisper
through the darkness,
"Are you asleep, Emily?"

"No," I whispered back.

"Me neither. I was thinking about Nina."

"I know. Me, too."
• • •

I heard Liz sigh. "I was so wrapped up in myself,
it never occurred to me Nina was counting on us
to be around this summer.
Did you know she felt that way?"

"No." I shook my head, angry with myself.
"I'd always go to her with my problems,
but it never occurred to me that she might be
having problems of her own."

I heard Liz snort. "What problems
do *you* have, Emily?"

Surprised by her remark
I said, "What?"

"Oh, sure, you and Nick broke up," she said.

I felt myself tense and I said stiffly,
"I know you don't like him."

"I never said that."

"Liz," I whispered fiercely, "don't you remember
bragging about how Marshall was so smart,
while poor Nick couldn't make it into
any AP classes?"

Liz was quiet for a moment,

then she said, "You're right, I did say that.
I'm sorry, Emily."
After another moment
she said, "I guess I was jealous."

I didn't think I'd heard correctly.
"What?" I said.

She sighed. "You want me to spell it out?
Okay. You're really smart and talented,
so artsy and cute . . .
Well, I can see why a guy
as good-looking as Nick
would be interested in you."

My head was spinning.
Liz was jealous of *me*?
She was the one I'd always envied,
with her assertiveness
and clear-headedness,
her way of always knowing
exactly what she wanted
and how to go after
and get it.

"And on top of everything," Liz was saying,
"you have these great parents,
a really sweet dad
and a mom
who's so devoted to you."

• • •

Could this be *Mama*
she was describing?
Genuinely curious, I asked,
"What do you mean?"

Liz expelled her breath
in an impatient huff. "Don't you know?
I'm talking about how she's always
cooking you your favorite dishes,
the way she can't get enough
of your paintings.
Your parents are so focused
on you, Emily."

"I guess so," I said slowly.
"But sometimes I think they're
too focused on me."

"That's not something I'd complain about,"
a new voice added from the dark.

"Nina?" I said. "You're not asleep?"

"Not anymore," she said, yawning. "You guys
are the loudest whisperers I've ever known."

"The loudest whisperers?" For some reason,
that struck me as extremely funny,
and I started to laugh.

• • •

"Emily's gone crazy," Liz said,
making me laugh even harder.
This made Nina laugh,
and soon Liz joined in.

When we finally quieted,
Liz said, "I say we go downstairs
and watch movies."

"Sounds good," I said.

"Is everyone ready?" Nina asked.
"I'm turning on the lights."
She flipped the switch
and I covered my eyes with my hands,
squeezing them shut
against the inevitable brightness.
As my eyes started to adjust,
I blinked against
black and red flowers
blooming in great irregular blobs
before my eyes.

Suddenly,
watching the wavering spots
dance and slowly begin
to fade away into the light,
it occurred to me

that I hadn't
really been seeing
my friends
fully before.
I'd always considered them
from only one perspective,
my own,
but there was so much more
to each of them
than I'd ever realized.

Perhaps the more familiar
someone is
to you,

the harder it is
to separate her from
the person she is
to you,
and the harder it is
to see her
as a person
in her own right.

Behind Glass

More than two months after the dance,
spring continues to bloom
with a burst of dogwood and azalea,

tulips opening up
their red and yellow throats
to the sky. Such glory
made me remember
Nick and me,
during the time
when we
were
we.

These days, whenever
I saw Nick
he was arm-in-arm
with Karen Malone,
a freshman.

Yesterday after school
I saw them, the sun throwing
a bright, ragged halo
over his hair, a breeze
ruffling her blouse,
the flash of his smile,
the thin, high notes
of her laughter.

As they walked away
I noticed the wind pushing
at my hair, saw the sun
glinting off the skin

of my arm.
How strange
to be noticing
these things,
but feeling them
no more
than if
I were
trapped behind
a pane
of glass.

III. *Taking Flight*

BUTCHER SHOP

Hanging from the rack,
five whole roast ducks, heads
balanced through wire loops, necks
arched graceful as flames,
bodies shining copper
under the fluorescent bulbs.
Rap of Little Aunt's knuckles against glass,
leaving a cloudy smudge
as she said, *"Na ge." That one.*
Second one from the right,
even I could see it was the fattest bird.

Light scattered up and down
the duck's gold-crisped skin
as the butcher lifted it swift and easy
from the wire to the block.

Musical *crack-thud* of the cleaver
biting through bone,
severing head,
metal on wood.
The butcher
swiped his damp brow
with his forearm, wiped
his hands across his stomach,
adding a fresh shine
to the blood-brown stains
mottling his apron.
When Little Aunt noticed the look
on my face, she frowned
and asked in Chinese,

"Don't you like duck?"

I shook my head, the motion
making the floor wriggle and hump.
"Are you okay?" Little Aunt asked,
and suddenly I felt as if
I were suffocating
in the dank heat,
island wet
sweat-slicking my hair to neck,
damp-beading my lip and nose,
face steaming, head
pulsing.
Little Aunt gripped
my shoulder as I swayed,

her fingers oily
against my sweat-wet arms.
"What's wrong with her?" the butcher asked,
gesturing with his cleaver.

"She's fine," Little Aunt said,
but he was still staring
so she said, *"She's overseas Chinese,
born in America."*
"Oh." The butcher nodded,
smack of cleaver to wood
as he cut up the duck, *smack.*
"Taiwan's hot, eh?" Little Aunt said. *"Are summers
hot in Virginia, too?"*
"Not this hot," I said.

"Wa! She's speaking English!"
the butcher said, so startled
he stopped chopping. *"That's English
she's speaking, isn't it?"*
Little Aunt nodded. *"It is."*
Smack and *crack* of cleaver
as the butcher cut up
the rest of the duck.
I prayed the rest of the summer
wouldn't be this hot
and wished
I could go back home.

• • •

"She's here for a visit?"
the butcher asked, scraping the duck
into an aluminum pan.
"That's right," Little Aunt said,
"This is her first week in Taipei
and she's here for the summer."
The butcher nodded his approval.
"It's good she came back. Back
to Taiwan." He fitted
a cardboard sheet over the pan,
pinching in its crinkled
metal edges, then waggled
a greasy finger at me
and said, *"You should practice*

your Chinese. After all, you're Chinese
and you should speak
Chinese."
His words were so much the same
as Baba's and Mama's,
I stared back at him.

The butcher spooned up
what looked like oil,
yellow bubbles lazily jostling
each other back and forth,
then poured it into
a small plastic cup. He capped
it tight and plunked it into
a plastic bag with the tray of duck,

then tied the bag
with a flourish, making
the plastic handles
rustle-flap.
"Senk yu," he said,
grinning and flashing
a gold tooth.
It wasn't until
we were nearly back at Little Aunt's
that I realized
what he was saying was,
Thank you.

Roast Duck Dinner

Steam rose from the bowl
of Chinese broccoli
sautéed crisp and fresh.
With my chopsticks I grasped
a few spears, blooming
emerald, touched
with buds,
and added them
to my rice.
"How is it?" Little Aunt asked in Chinese.
"It's delicious!"
And it was.
Little Aunt's cooking

reminded me of Mama's.
"Na li, na li," she demurred
when I told her so.
"Your mother is a very good cook,"
she said, smiling.
"Have some duck."
She poured oily glaze
over the plate
piled high with crisp-skinned duck,
then lifted a piece in her chopsticks
and nudged it into
my bowl.

The brown-skinned duck

glistened, its sweet
meaty scent
wafting up
from my bowl.
I bit into
the roast meat,
tasting
tender flesh, teeth
sinking into
fat-rich skin.
A bit of oil trickled
slick and sticky
from the corner
of my mouth.

• • •

Embarrassed, I glanced
at Little Aunt,
but she didn't
notice. She was
hunched over the chunk
of bone
in her hand, fingers
greased
from the meat,
lips snarled back
as she tugged and gnawed
with teeth,
doggedly working
the flesh
off of bone.   213 ⌐

Just as I was thinking
this was the same way Baba and Mama
ate roast duck, and
wondering
if that was how I looked
eating it, too,
I remembered the way
the whole ducks looked
hanging in the butcher window,
staring at nothing
with eyes burned away
to nubs,
gaping with beaks

rigid as skeleton
teeth,
and suddenly the
butcher-shop nausea
was back.
Bell-like
thunk
of the part-gnawed
chunk of bone
plunking
back down
into my bowl.

"So tomorrow . . ."
I looked up and Little Aunt
patted her mouth clean
with a napkin
and said, *". . . you'll start*
your Chinese class
at Taiwan Normal University,
your mama's alma mater."
Little Aunt studied me,
frowned a little, and said,
"Does that sound all right?"
I took a sip of water, clean and cool,
and the nausea lifted a bit
but still lingered
like a persistent smell.
Little Aunt kept looking at me, worried,

so I forced a smile and said,
"That sounds fine."

COMFORTER

Coming upstairs after dinner,
I turned on the light
and saw a splash of red and orange,
poppies blooming across
the creamy expanse of comforter
covering my bed at Little Aunt's.
Its pattern was so much like
a quilt we had at home
I felt a jolt of recognition
warming into pleased surprise.

I ran my hand over
the comforter's cool cotton
and fingered the ridge of a seam.
I imagined I smelled a trace
of Mama's face cream,
and for a moment I was a child,
sitting cross-legged on my parents' bed,
feeling the softness
of my pajamas against
my skin still damp from my bath,
and enjoying the rhythmic strokes
as Mama combed out my hair.

• • •

As I listened to
the metallic *chit*
of the clock on the dresser,
a longing for home came over me,
sharp and unexpected
as a jerk of the comb
against a tangle
in my hair.
Mama would always
work the snarl loose,
slowly teasing out each strand
until the comb pulled smoothly through.

The last thing I remembered
before falling asleep at night
was the feel of the comb
stroking down my scalp,
the smell of my just-washed hair,
and the touch of Mama's hand on my head
as she'd give me a little pat
and say, *"Hao le. Qu shui ba."*
There we go. Time for bed now.

CHINESE CLASS

The next morning,
Little Aunt called a cab

to take me to Chinese class.
On the way, the driver asked me about the class
and how I liked Taipei thus far.
I understood everything he said,
but the words I wanted to say in response
were slow to come.
My Chinese felt awkward;
the tones and sounds
were ones I wasn't used to handling.

It felt something like
putting your feet into
a new pair of shoes
you try on in the store.
You're unused to the stiffness
that changes your gait,
throwing off the way
you roll your foot from heel to toe,
and making you suddenly aware
of the process of walking,
one you've taken for granted for so many years
you'd forgotten it was a skill
you once had to learn.

By the time we arrived at my class,
I was feeling pleased with my ability
to carry on a simple conversation in Chinese.
I counted out the proper amount
of *tai bi* dollars for fare and tip,

then paid the driver
and said, *"Xie xie."*
He acknowledged my thanks with a nod
and then he said something
I couldn't quite make out.
It was only after he drove away
that I realized what he'd said
to me was, *"Arigato."*
The driver must have thought
that I spoke Chinese
the way that I did
because I was
Japanese.

SPEAKING THE LANGUAGE

Uh-huh, Uh-uh.
Mmm-hmmm, Mmm-mmmm.
Djeet? Yeah, djoo?
Mama told me how hard English was
for her to understand
when she first came to America.
The formal English
she'd learned from her textbooks
was so different from the way Americans spoke.
She'd learned *yes* and *no*,
Have you eaten your dinner yet?
and *Yes, thank you. And yourself?*

• • •

But the words she heard instead
were hard to grasp, slippery
as so many small fish
darting here and there,
shining slips of color
with movements so quick,
impossible to catch.
Try as you might to follow one fish,
another glides right past,
confusing your eye
so the first is lost
somewhere among
the whole, swirling group—
here for a moment
then swimming away
into the wide ocean
and gone.

Shi de, bu shi.
Ni chi le fan mei you? Wo chi le, ni ne?
I practice saying to myself,
Yes, no.
Have you eaten yet? Yes, how about you?

In my mind, the words slip easily,
casually from my tongue.
I hear the way
even the youngest children

unthinkingly toss out
these simple phrases,
the sounds and tones rolling lazily,
saucily from their mouths,
the unconscious music
of everyday Chinese
sung out through
the streets of Taipei.

Mama and Baba say
I used to speak beautiful Chinese,
my accent clear
and the tones perfect.
But then when I started kindergarten,
I remember how the other kids laughed
at the way I couldn't understand
any English at all.
Mama says it wasn't long
before I spoke English
exactly like my classmates.
But she said I refused
to speak Chinese anymore.
Even at home
with just Baba and Mama
and no one else to hear,
they spoke Chinese to me
and I answered them
in English.

• • •

Now when I open my mouth
to speak Chinese
the words stumble out,
dissonant and harsh
as a series of misplayed notes.
Like a beginning musician
violating all rules
I go back and try to correct,
inevitably hitting
the same wrong notes again.
By then the easy rhythm,
the back-and-forth flow
of conversation is gone,
irretrievably lost,
broken by me and my
tone-deaf, tuneless,
off-key imitation
of Chinese.

I'm getting used to
the look on people's faces
when I try to speak with them.
Surprise, then confusion
turning to befuddlement
or plain curiosity
as they ask, *Xiao Jie,*
Ni shi na li ren?
Where are you from, Miss?

•   •   •

Now I wonder:
How many times
must Mama have heard
this question,
Where are you from, dear?
And did they ever ask,
Are you Chi-nese, Japa-nese
or what?

FEELING AT HOME

I walked down the sidewalk along *Luo-si-fu* Road
during the late afternoon rush,

shopping for gifts.
For Liz I'd bought a silk scarf
embroidered with chrysanthemums.
Then I stopped
at a street vendor's stall
and opened a sandalwood fan,
feeling the tassel at its bottom
brush against my skin,
cool and soft.
I admired the light-colored wood,
each panel carved with birds and flowers,
and the vendor urged me to try it out.
As I fanned myself she said,
"Ni wen wen kan?" *Doesn't it smell sweet?*
The breeze from the fan

smelled of sandalwood.
I decided to buy it for Nina.

After paying the vendor
and putting the fan in my bag,
I settled it over my shoulder,
then rejoined the throng
of pedestrian traffic,
women toting their groceries home
in pink-and-white-striped plastic bags,
business people clad in suits or dresses
striding purposefully past,
and students wearing white shirts
with navy blue pants or skirts,
laughing and chatting as they walked arm-in-arm
in clusters of two or three.

There was a certain strangeness
to seeing everywhere
people who looked enough like me
from the outside
that you might not be able
to single me out
from the bustling crowd.
You wouldn't guess
that the girl who'd lived her whole life
in a country on the other side of the world
would be me.
The thought that I might be

the only one
among all of these people
to be thinking such thoughts
made me feel
suddenly
alone
even in the midst
of such movement and noise,
the mechanical roar of motors idling,
exhaust fumes drifting up
in scraggly black curls from the street,
the angry buzzing here and there
of a motorcycle or car
gunning its engine, impatient

for the light to change.

I checked my watch,
thinking it was time to head back.
I pulled out my map of the city
and saw I was still blocks away
from the nearest bus stop.
I became suddenly aware
of the afternoon heat, relentless
as a giant hand
pushing down on my head
with a slow steady pressure,
and I felt a bit faint.
I stumbled a little,
almost bumping into someone

who'd stopped on the sidewalk in front of me.
I caught myself just in time
and looked up to see a woman
holding a toddler balanced on her hip.
I apologized and asked
if she and the little girl
were all right.

The woman smiled and assured me
they were fine.
She returned her attention
to a table stacked with books for sale
outside the bookstore
on the corner where we stood.
A wail of protest
came from the little girl;
her mother shifted her to the other hip
and jiggled her up and down,
but the little girl shook her head,
wriggled in her mother's arms
and began to wail louder.

"Mei-mei, Let Mama look at the books,"
said the woman,
but her daughter's face puckered
and she started to cry.
"Don't cry," her mother said,
repositioning her. *"Let's sing."*

•   •   •

She began to sing a tune
so familiar
I could almost hear my own mother
singing, too:
The sun goes down the mountain,
but tomorrow morning it will climb up again . . .
It was a folk song,
one Mama used to sing me
when I was a child.
Flowers fade, but next year
they will bloom again.
As I listened to the song,
the words echoed in my head,
and before I knew what I was doing

I opened my mouth
and began to sing, too:
The pretty little bird flies away
but it's not coming back.
My green spring like the little bird
will not return,
My green spring like the little bird
will not return.
Bie di na ya you, Bie di na ya you . . .

When we finished the song,
the woman smiled at me
then said to her daughter,
"It's getting late. Shall we go home now?"
The girl nodded

and her mother said
with a nod in my direction,
"Tell Jie-Jie thank you for the song."

The girl hid her face
against her mother's shoulder,
too shy to say anything to me,
but as they walked away
she waved good-bye.
I waved back
and she smiled
and kept waving to me
as her mother carried her
down the street.
Just before her mother turned the corner
and they were out of sight,
the little girl called out,
"Xie xie, Jie-Jie,"
Thank you, Big Sister.

MISSING NICK

There were no empty seats on the bus back
to Little Aunt's house,
so I stood in the aisle
near a seat occupied by a teenaged couple,
sitting close to each other
and holding hands.

•   •   •

Despite the close-pressing crowd during rush hour
and the exhaust-choked air, muggy
with late afternoon heat,
the noise of the bus shifting gears,
the periodic squealing of brakes
as it slowed down
then jerked to a stop,
the boy and girl
noticed only
each other.

I remembered sitting with Nick that way,
waiting for the start of a movie,
our hands joined,
the warmth of his arm
intertwined with my own,
our shared armrest
cool beneath my elbow
as the theater darkened
and we snuggled down
into our seats
together.

Just before the movie began,
I watched Nick unwrap
a chocolate kiss,
carefully lifting the candy
free from its shiny nest.

Holding it between
his thumb and forefinger,
he gave me a smile,
then brought the kiss to my mouth.
Even now, I could feel
the butterfly touch
of his fingers
to my lips,
and the way the candy
slowly dissolved
into a mass of sweetness
on my tongue.

A sudden surge of wanting
came over me,
strong as a wave
crashing over my head,
throwing me down,
salt water burning through
my nose and throat,
the stinging of sand particles sharp
as so many tiny bits of glass,
miniature mirrors
throwing needlelike rays of sun
into my weeping eyes.

THE PAINTING

The pretty little bird flies away
but it's not coming back . . .
As I ate dinner with Little Aunt,
I thought about the little girl
and her song.
Later, as I washed the dishes,
snatches of song
echoed in my mind.
I could hear the little girl's mother
and my own voice singing, too,
but the sound that rang out
most clearly in my mind
was the music of
Mama's voice singing
and I realized how much
I missed
her and Baba.

I wondered
what it must have been like
for my parents
while they were growing up
here in Taipei.
I tried to imagine
Baba as an elementary school student
with a khaki green satchel
slung over his shoulder

or Mama as a toddler
in her mother's arms,
but the images were hazy,
refusing to focus
in my mind.
It occurred to me then
I'd never seen a photograph
of either of my parents
as children.

So after I finished with the dishes
I walked down the hall
to Little Aunt's room
and knocked on her door.
When she answered my knock
I asked if she had any photos
of my parents as children.

*"As children? I don't think so . . .
But maybe from their college
or graduate school days.
Come in while I take a look."*

I hadn't been inside
Little Aunt's room before.
I caught a glimpse
of a neat room, simply furnished,
before I stepped inside.
That was when

I saw the painting
that hung on her wall:

Lotus leaves cupped
like large, deep-green bowls,
their edges fanning out wide
like the brims of upturned
velvet hats, their tips flirtatiously
curled here and there
as if a breeze
were passing through.
A single lotus pod
showed off its circular pattern
of seed pockets plump

as a cat's paw pads,
the seeds nearly ready
to slip from the hull.

Starring the painting
in a wavy bright line
were the lotus flowers—
a few fat buds
rosy with the promise
of the blooms to come,
the mature flowers bursting
with red-tipped petals
tender and inviting
as the leaves
of a ripe artichoke.

Flying in the sky
above the lotus
were the swallows,
three black birds
with throats tinted orange
and wings streaming back
in graceful points
echoed by their long dark tails,
sharply forked
like fishes' tails,
their motions so fluid
the swallows appeared
to be swimming
through air.

Little Aunt brought me
out of the painting
when she closed the drawer
where she'd been looking for photos
and said, *"Here they are."*

But instead of taking the photos,
I pointed to the painting on the wall
and said, "Who is the artist
who painted this painting?"

Little Aunt gave me a questioning look,
then said, *"Don't you know?*

*It was painted by
your mother."*

Mama painted this painting?
At first I couldn't
believe what I'd heard,
but another part of me
was already thinking,
Of course. Who else could have
painted it?

For the first time I focused
on the Chinese characters
written with fine brushstrokes
along the painting's left edge.
I recognized a few words,
hua, for flower
yan, for swallow
and *Xu Lan,* my mother's name
before she was married.

I should have seen it
all along—
her strong brushstrokes,
the warmth of the colors,
and more than anything else,
the care with which
she painted the finest details,
the slim soft hairs

making up each feather,
the veins on the petals
in each tight bud.

Looking at Mama's painting,
I suddenly realized
her birthday was coming up
next month.
It would be the first time
I wouldn't be there
to celebrate with her and Baba.

Always on her birthday,
Baba and I would prepare
traditional birthday noodles,

unbroken strands to symbolize a full, long life.
Though we used her recipe for handmade noodles
with slices of mushrooms and cabbage
and slivers of mustard greens and pork,
somehow it never tasted the same
as when Mama cooked this dish for us.
The noodles Baba and I made
weren't quite so tender,
they were missing a certain *jin xing*,
or *springiness to the dough*,
but Mama would always smile
and pronouce the noodles
zhen hao chi, truly delicious.

• • •

I imagined Mama's face
in the glow of the candles
we'd light on her cake in the evening,
but my parents seemed so far away
in memory, time, and space
the image seemed
to recede in my mind,
as though I were peering at it
through the wrong end of a telescope.

I looked back up
at Mama's painting
and somehow, the colors of the lotus—
the pink and white of the flowers,
the dark green of the leaves—
brought me back
to the memory of Mama's birthday cake,
Baba and I singing
Zhu ni sheng ri kuai le,
Happy birthday to you,
and Mama's smile,
then, just before she blew out
the three candles on her cake,
Mama's voice, full of warmth, as she said
the same as she did every year,
Xie xie, Lao-Gong,
Xie xie, Nu-Er,
Thank you, Husband,
Thank you, Daughter.

SAILING FOR AMERICA

The young woman
in the photograph
wore a rose-colored *qi-pao*,
a long Chinese dress
with a slit at the ankles.
Looking at this picture,
I was struck by
her features and expression
and I saw how much
she looked like me.

It was Mama, of course,
looking into the distance
on a day so bright
she'd lifted a hand
to shade her face.
The beginnings of a smile
played on her lips
and a breeze ruffled her hair.
Little Aunt said this photo was taken
when Mama finished college.
She was twenty-two,
six years older than I am now,
when she sailed from her home in Taiwan
to America for graduate school.

I imagined her standing on the deck,

balanced against the sway of waves,
feet poised in a T, heel of her right foot
tucked toward the inside arch of the left
in the most graceful position
for standing in a *qi-pao*
with torso turned out slightly.
The curve of her calf
would be hidden by the dress
until my mother took a step
or shifted her weight
and the folds of rose silk
fluttered apart
at the low slit above each ankle
then fell back in place

as she straightened
with a scrape of the heels
of her patent black pumps
against the rolling wooden planks.

I could almost feel the salt breeze
teasing her dark, wavy hair,
styled like *Au-de-li* Hepburn's
in *Roman Holiday.*
Perhaps that day
the ship's captain,
a friend of my grandfather,
passed her a red-cheeked apple he'd saved
and waved away her thanks, saying,
"I promised your father to take good care of you."

• • •

How did that apple taste
as my mother bit through the smooth,
shiny skin and crunched into sweet,
white meat? Perhaps
she licked a stray drop of juice
from her knuckle,
tasting ocean
and in that moment
of sweetness and brine
my mother looked out
over the endlessly waving sea
scattered with diamonds of light
and imagined the shores
of America.   239 ⁓

CALLING ALEX

Seeing Mama's painting
made me think about
painting again,
myself.

But before I took brush to palette
I wanted to gather fresh images
and see more artwork,
even to discuss the art I saw
with another artist,

and I thought of Alex.
He'd given me his parents' number in Taipei
before the end of school,
when I told him I'd be here
this summer, too.

"Emily," he said when I called.
"How *are* you?"
The gladness in his voice
reached me through the telephone line,
palpable like a ball
someone tosses to you
as you watch it become
steadily larger, a perfect sphere

soaring through the air
toward you.

Alex said he'd thought of me
when he visited the National Palace Museum
a few weeks ago. When he asked me
if I'd like to go with him again
I said I would, feeling pleased
as if I'd reached up
and caught the ball
square in my hand.
I imagined pulling back
my shoulder and arm
and feeling the pleasant
stretch of muscles

in a motion so familiar,
the fluid gesture
of throwing the ball
right back.

SHAVED ICE

Alex and I decided to meet at
a *bing guo dian, an iced treat shop,*
before heading over to the museum.
I arrived a few minutes early at the shop,
and found a free table.
I sat down and breathed in
the heavenly scent
of air-conditioning,
its lovely chill
on my street-hot skin.
Smells of pineapple,
mango and papaya,
tropical flavors mixing
with the aroma of sweet milk
wafting irresistibly through the air.

Tinkle-ting of the bell atop the door
announcing an entrance;
it was Alex.
"You're here already!" he said.
"Have you been waiting very long?"

His words were courteous,
almost formal,
but his voice was bright
and his smile so glad
I found myself smiling back.
"Alex," I said, "it's great to see you."

"Are you hungry?" he asked.
"What would you like to eat?"
Just then from behind the counter
the buzz of a metal saw
biting down deep into
a great bluish block
of ice. Maniacal
whine of blade
to block, slivers
of ice piling high,
falling like fresh snow
onto the plates.

"What's that?" I asked, pointing.

"Bao bing," Alex said. *Shaved ice.*
"It's very good. Would you like to try some?

I nodded *yes*
just as a waitress came over
to take our order.
Alex asked her a question

and I was surprised to hear
how different he sounded in Chinese,
speaking smoothly
and with a certain authority,
his accent refined
and his voice expressive.

Just then the waitress
turned to me and asked
what toppings I'd like.
Suddenly
I couldn't bear
to have Alex hear me
speaking Chinese,
my words clumsy and slow
and marked by a foreign accent.
After a silence
I said in English to Alex,
"I can't order in Chinese."

Alex nodded and said,
"Tell me what toppings you'd like,
and I'll translate for the waitress."
I picked pineapple pieces
sharp and sunny;
purple chunks of taro
tender as baked yams;
green beans sweet
as new peas.

. . .

Before long, the waitress
brought us our plates,
chilly and heaped treasure-high.
After the first shivery bites of ice,
my taste buds came alive
as I licked from the spoon
a drop of sweet milk
pooled blue-white
in the dip of its belly.

Watching me Alex smiled
and asked, "Do you like it?"
I nodded. As I smiled back
my teeth chattered a little
from the ice and we laughed.

I was nearly through with my plate,
the ice flakes mostly melted,
tapioca pearls starring the sludgy ice
like pink and white flowers,
green beans peeking through
the soupy wet here and there,
when the waitress came by
to ask if we wanted
anything else.

I shook my head;
Alex thanked her

and asked for the check.
Listening to him speak Chinese,
his tenor voice
melodic and rich
like the tones of a bamboo flute,
I wished my own Chinese
had half
the music of his.
Though Chinese was
my mother tongue,
English was
my native
tongue
and I didn't quite feel
I fit in,
either here in Taipei
or even in Virginia,
where I'd lived
all my life
until now.

The waitress returned
to take our plates,
and before giving her mine
I took a final bite,
my teeth slicing into
a piece of grass jelly,
slightly bitter
like dark chocolate

with high notes
wild and sweet,
and that moment I knew
my universe was richer
with the music
of two languages,
the rhythms
of two cultures
and the flavors
of both
my worlds.

BECOMING DRAGON

At the National Palace Museum,
Alex showed me two of his favorites
from the jade collection.
The first was a Ch'ing Dynasty work,
Jadeite Cabbage with Insects.
It was carved from a piece of bi-colored jade,
milk white on the sides and bottom
and a rich emerald green on top—
the bok choy cabbage leaves
emerged smooth and white
along the head's length
before their hue changed
to a bright jewel green
coloring their curly tips.

Perched atop the leaves
and looking as if they might hop away
at any moment
were a katydid
and a locust
carved from the same
deep green.

"Can you imagine," I said to Alex,
"the artist, one hundred years ago—
holding this piece of uncut jade,
studying its colors,
and seeing in the green and white
a head of bok choy
and two insects?"

Alex smiled at me and said,
"I thought you might like it."

We then went to see a Han Dynasty work,
Jade Cup in the Shape of an Animal Horn,
carved from a piece of white jade
with undertones of brown and green.
On one side of the vessel
a dragon twined
his serpentine body
in a graceful S
from top to bottom.
On the other side,

a phoenix wound
her body down
in the shape of an S,
her tail curving toward
the base of the cup
where it met the round coil
of the dragon's tail.

This carving brought to mind
a set of rice bowls we used at home.
With a thin gold line
brightening its rim,
each bowl was etched on one side
with the design of a dragon,
and patterned on the other
with the form of a phoenix.
My favorite was always
the phoenix,
a creature whose features resembled
those of various birds.
Her colorful peacock's feathers
waved out in graceful swirls
from her body, slender and lithe
like a mandarin duck's,
and her great dark eyes
seemed to gaze back at me
so knowingly
and with such friendliness;
I recalled the way

I wanted my bowl turned
so that I could see
the phoenix as I ate.
Mama would always turn my bowl
with the phoenix facing me.
Then she'd smile and say, "The phoenix
will bring you luck, Emily."

Now to Alex I said,
"My mother says
the phoenix is a sign
of good things to come."

Alex smiled and said,
"That's right."

I was admiring the scroll
of the dragon's back
and the lift of his tail
when he added,
"My mother likes this piece
very much, too."
Noticing the way
his face brightened
when he mentioned her,
I said, "You seem very happy
to be back with your parents."

"Yes," Alex said. "I am."

Hearing the sincerity in his voice,
I thought of the resentment,
even anger I'd been feeling
toward my own parents
before I left for Taipei
and I felt a twinge
of regret, perhaps,
or even guilt.

"Alex," I said, "you're very Chinese."
He gave me a questioning look
and I explained, "What I mean is that
you appreciate your parents."

Alex smiled and said, "I'm sure
you appreciate your parents, too."

"Actually," I said, "I think
I could appreciate them more.
I wish I were more like you in that way."

"It's different for me," he said,
"because I don't see my parents
as often as I'd like."
He looked at the jade cup
for a moment then said,
"When I first came back
to Taipei last month
my mother said I'd grown taller

since the last time she saw me."
He smiled and continued,
"But I don't think
I could have grown very much
in just two months.
I think she was remembering me
as younger than I actually am."
He looked back at me
and said, "It's funny.
To you, I seem very Chinese,
but my parents think I've become
very American."

"In what way do they think
you're American?"

Alex considered the question,
then said, "Mainly, they believe
I've become very independent.
I think my mother, in particular,
feels I'm growing up
more quickly than she'd like."

His words made me think of
my own mother and I said quietly,
"That must be hard for her."

He nodded. "I think it is.
But she tries to make the best of things.

I overheard her tell my father . . ." He paused
then said, "I'm trying to think
of how to translate it to English."

Impulsively, I said, "Tell me in Chinese."

Alex looked surprised.
"I didn't know you knew Chinese."

"I don't know it very well," I said.
"But I'm trying to improve."

"'*Mei ban fa. Wang zi cheng long,*'" he said.
"Did you understand that?"

"Your mother said, 'There's no help for it.'
But what does '*wang zi cheng long*' mean?"

"That's the part I was trying to translate.
It's a saying that expresses the hope
of Chinese parents
that their sons will one day
become dragons,
and that their daughters will become
phoenixes. This means
they want their children to grow up
to achieve their fullest potential."

As I considered this,

I understood Alex's mother was saying
that she accepted the inevitable
yet wished for the best,
every imaginable blessing
for her son.
To Alex I said, smiling,
"Your mother hopes
you'll become a dragon."

Alex smiled back. "Isn't that
every mother's hope for her child?"
He looked back at the dragon
carved into the jade
and his face as he studied it
became solemn, calm.
He blinked, then removed his glasses,
rubbing his temples
and the bridge of his nose.
I'd never seen Alex
without his glasses,
and before he replaced them I saw
a certain strength
to his features
I'd never noticed before.
I had the sense Alex would be ready
to meet whatever difficulties
might lie ahead of him,
facing them with his usual
quiet dignity.

• • •
Then, feeling as if
I had inadvertently glimpsed
something private,
I looked away
and focused my attention
on the dragon cup, allowing its colors
to draw me in.
The jade shone a golden white,
glimmering pale green
here and there;
flecks of light brown
marked the dragon's brow
and a spot of dark brown
shadowed a curl in his tail.
Light touched his wide snout
and flickered at the tip
of his pointed tongue,
and for a moment it seemed
to gleam in his eyes.
I wondered what wisdom
might yet be
alive in him now,
perhaps two thousand years
after the artist awakened him
from the luminous jade
where he'd slept, unnoticed
and unformed,
until the first sharp cuts

of chisel into stone
brought him into sharp relief
and he emerged,
head and claws, back and tail—
cheng long,
becoming dragon.

LIKE NICK

Later that week
I was walking into the library
at the American Embassy,
when I saw a boy
at one of the tables
push his fingers back
through wheat-pale hair
in a familiar gesture
that made my heart
beat wildly.

Nick? Here, in Taipei?
Even as I felt
a buzz of anticipation
rising up to meet
the old gladness,
there was something else,
a hesitation
bordering on restraint,

almost as if I were
watching myself from afar
and telling my other self,
Wait.

Just then the boy turned
his face toward me
and I saw
it wasn't Nick after all.
This boy looked older than him
by a couple of years,
and his face was sharper,
his look more serious
than the way I remembered Nick.

When I saw it wasn't him,
I braced myself
for the inevitable pang
of wanting,
the emptiness as if
I'd lost something
irretrievably precious.
But instead there was
only a twinge,
a slight ache that reminded me
of losing a tooth.

I remembered the way
I'd push my tongue against

the loosening baby tooth,
testing how far
it would go,
and stopping only
at the point of pain.
The ache
grew a little less
each day,
and the tooth gave way
more and more,
until finally
it toppled free.

Probing the sharp points
of the roots of the fallen tooth,
I would realize with a kind
of wondering surprise
that the pain was completely gone,
leaving behind
only the smoothness
of a brand new gap
in my teeth.

The boy who looked like Nick
pushed his chair back,
pulled his backpack over his shoulder,
and headed for the door.
As he walked past me,
he caught my glance,

and we exchanged
the slightly awkward smiles
of strangers whose eyes
happen to meet.

I thought about
the little girl
I once was,
carefully placing
the fallen baby tooth
under my pillow
at night,
the way I'd look
with some sadness

at the small
pearl of a tooth,
knowing I wouldn't
be seeing it again.

Pushing my tongue
against the new smoothness,
the gap I was learning
to know,
I understood
that it was only a matter of time
before a new tooth would grow
in the place of the one
I'd lost.

GIFTS

My last week in Taipei
I still hadn't found
a gift to bring home for Mama,
so after my final Chinese class
I went out to look once more.
I walked across *Shi Da* Road
to an art supply store I'd noticed before.

I made my way through the store
until I found the paintbrushes.
I fingered one brush's bristles,
arranged in an arch
and spreading out
from the handle
like a fan.
I touched
the soft white hairs
protruding from the handle
of another brush
in a puff round and fat
as a rabbit's tail.

I chose an assortment of brushes,
a wide one for painting
great sweeps of water or air,
a slender brush
with fine hairs for painting

the smallest details,
and brushes of all sizes
and shapes in between.
I found pads of paper,
ink blocks and inkstone,
small colored squares of pigment
from teal green and red
to yellow and cerulean blue—
everything Mama might need
for Chinese painting.

When I left the store
my bag was heavy
with the satisfying weight
of my gift for Mama.

I thought I'd stroll and window shop
before heading back to Little Aunt's house.
I bought a chunk of sugarcane
to chew on as I walked,
my jaws and teeth working
the coarse fibers
as I gnawed the hard, pulpy mass
until it softened
and I sucked in sharp
sweet juice.

Wishing I'd worn a hat
I squinted against the sun,

then ducked into the tepid shade
of a vendor's canopy.
I noticed a collection of small jade figures,
looked closer and recognized
the twelve animals of the Chinese zodiac:
rat, ox, tiger, rabbit, dragon, snake,
horse, ram, monkey, rooster, dog, boar.
I stroked the back of the tiger,
fingering the cuts in the jade
representing his stripes.
Next I picked up
the monkey, admiring
the curl of her tail.
I'd decided to buy
these two for myself,
when the dragon
caught my eye.
His body twined
like a serpent's
and clouds spiraled
in little twists
from his back
as though he had just
flown down from the sky.

Holding the dragon
I thought of Alex.
We were nearly through
painting the mural

and when we finished I wanted
to give him something,
to thank him for painting with me
and to let him know
how glad I was
to know him.
Perhaps later
when I knew him better
I might even tell him
how he'd helped me
to get to know
myself
a little more, too.

262   I set down the three figures,
tiger, monkey, and dragon
and told the vendor
I wanted to look around more
before buying them.
She nodded and I turned
to a mirrored rack
flashing colored plastic,
glittering metals,
row upon row
of sunglasses to try.

I slipped on a pair
of cat's-eye glasses
and the vendor said,

"Hao piao liang." How pretty.
She nodded at me from the shade
of her beribboned straw hat,
her face wrinkling in a smile,
the ends of the ribbon
tied under her chin
fluttering a little
with the movement.
"This pair?" I asked her
pointing to the sunglasses
and ready to ask the price
when she said,
*"No, not the glasses,
you. Any pair you pick
will look good."*

263 ⌒

For a moment I was startled
until I realized
she was only trying
to sell sunglasses.
I smiled back at her,
then looked out toward the street
and for a moment
I saw Taipei
bathed in a warm sepia glow:
bustling crowds of people,
whizzing cars, motorcycles
buzzing like mosquitos,
buildings blazing
under the afternoon sun,

trees rustling their leaves
in the shimmering waves
of heat pulsing through the air.

I added the sunglasses
to my purchases,
then before I set back out
I looked back and caught
a glimpse of my face
in the small square of mirror
atop the rack of glasses.
I saw a girl
looking pleased
with the gifts she'd found,
thinking of her friends
and family at home.
She looked happy,
relaxed
even pretty,
just as the vendor
had said.

BECOMING PHOENIX

My final night in Taipei
I finished packing my suitcase,
then went to bed
and slept.
In my dreams I heard

a drowsy music
like the murmuring of rain.
Growing louder,
the sound became
a high sweet singing
as if a songbird were perched
near my windowsill.

I turned toward the music
to see a winged creature
rustling her peacock-bright feathers.
She lifted her golden pheasant's head,
slender throat pulsing
as she finished her song,
then stretched her great wings
and stepped toward me
on legs like a crane's,
elegant and tall.
As she cocked her head to the side,
peering at me with one bright eye,
I recognized her—
sovereign of birds
and empress of the air.

As she gazed at me
I felt a warmth suffuse me,
as if I'd stepped out into the sun
on a mild April afternoon.
It was as if the breeze

had carried over a familiar scent,
something like the way Mama smelled
when she'd gather me into her arms
after I'd fallen
when I was a child
playing outside.

Mama would brush away
dirt and grass from my clothes,
wipe away my tears,
look me over for bruises,
then clean and bandage my cuts.

Sometimes even if I wasn't hurt
I'd linger for a moment,
wanting Mama to hold me again,
and she would.
Then with a final pat
she'd send me to play.
I'd turn in the doorway
before going outside
to see Mama smile and wave,
then I'd run back out
into the sun.

Now as I drowsed,
basking in the creature's brilliance,
her light shining over me
like the sun in spring,

and smelling her fragrance
like Mama's own scent,
I sensed her impatience
to rise up and fly.

"Don't go," I begged her.
"Or if you must go,
take me with you."
She laughed
with a sound low and sweet
as the cooing of doves
as if to say,
I am you.

With her image alive in my mind,
I awoke the next morning,
so early it was still cool.
By the time Little Aunt
would drive me to the airport,
the day would be steamy and hot.
I didn't mind;
I knew I'd be boarding the plane
and flying home.
I couldn't wait to see Baba and Mama
and Nina, Liz, and Alex;
I wanted to return
to painting the mural.
In my heart I saw
the final creature I would paint:

rising above the monkey and tiger,
reigning over
the birds and the trees—
the phoenix
spreading her wings,
ready to fly.

About the Author

Like Emily, Joyce Lee Wong has lived in Richmond and spent time in Taiwan, where she took Chinese classes and taught English. She is a graduate of the University of Virginia Law School and now lives in California with her husband and two young children. This is her first book.

This book was designed by Jay Colvin and art directed by Becky Terhune. It is set in Adobe Garamond, a typeface that is based on those created in the sixteenth century by Claude Garamond. Garamond modeled his typefaces on those created by Venetian printers at the end of the fifteenth century. The modern version used in this book was designed by Robert Slimbach, who studied Garamond's historic typefaces at the Plantin-Moretus Museum in Antwerp, Beligium.